the importance of
wings

Its the flash addiction
for me

the importance of wings

Robin Friedman

Charlesbridge

Published by Charlesbridge
85 Main Street
Watertown, MA 02472
(617) 926-0329
www.charlesbridge.com

Library of Congress Cataloging-in-Publication Data
Friedman, Robin, 1968–
    The importance of wings/ Robin Friedman.
      p. cm.
    Summary: Although she longs to be an all-American girl, timid, thirteen-year-old,
Israeli-born Roxanne, who idolizes Wonder Woman, begins to see things differently
when the supremely confident Liat, also from Israel, moves into the "cursed house"
next door and they become friends.
    ISBN 978-1-58089-330-5 (reinforced for library use)
    ISBN 978-1-58089-331-2 (softcover)
    ISBN 978-1-60374-504-6 (ebook)
    ISBN 978-1-60734-265-6 (ebook pdf)
[1. Self-confidence—Fiction. 2. Self-perception—Fiction. 3. Identity—Fiction.
4. Loss (Psychology)—Fiction. 5. Friendship—Fiction. 6. Sisters—Fiction.
7. Israelis—United States—Fiction. 8. Staten Island (New York, N.Y.)—History—
20th century—Fiction.] I. Title.
PZ7.F89785 Im 2009
[Fic]—dc22   2008025326

Printed in the United States of America
(hc) 10 9 8 7 6 5 4 3 2 1
(sc) 10 9 8 7 6 5 4 3 2 1

Display type and text type set in Stereo HiFi and Adobe Caslon Pro
Printed by Berryville Graphics in Berryville, Virginia, USA
Color separations by Coral Graphic Services, Inc., in Hicksville, New York, USA
Production supervision by Brian G. Walker
Designed by Diane M. Earley
Paperback cover design by Sarah Richards Taylor

For my Israeli-American family:
my generous mother, Sarah;
my wise father, Daniel;
my beautiful sister, Galit;
and my sweet brother, Jonathan.

chapter one

it's called the cursed house because something terrible always happens to anyone who lives there.

It's not a scary or ugly house, like those haunted houses you see in the movies, but it is different. It's the biggest house on the block, and the only one painted bright pink. And the backyard leads to the woods, which are scary. Nobody else's house leads to the woods.

My sister, Gayle, and I are walking home from school when we see the sign:

House for Sale
Contact Appleseed Agency

Neither of us says anything. Finally Gayle asks, "What kind of weird name is Appleseed?"

"I dunno," I reply. "Maybe it's . . ." But I trail off, because I can't think of an explanation. We stare at it for a few more seconds in silence, then finally start for our house.

Gayle walks straight into the kitchen, turns on the TV, and gets out the cereal. "Do you think anyone will buy it, Roxanne?" she asks as she dumps a rushing stream of Cocoa Pebbles into her bowl.

"Yeah, I guess so," I say. I make sure the TV is tuned to Channel 5, which shows the best reruns after school.

We sit at the kitchen table watching TV and eating cereal, but my mind drifts from *The Brady Bunch* to the Cursed House. I think about all the awful stories we've heard about the people who lived there—like the one about Stood-Up Serena. Stood-Up Serena was a high school senior who was stood up by her date on the night of the senior prom. She walked into the woods in her lavender prom gown and never came back.

Then there was the time the FBI swarmed over the house in the middle of the night with flashlights and guns. The family who lived there got busted for something major, but no one ever found out what.

Four months later, the Brinns moved in. They were there only a week when their youngest daughter fell down the stairs and broke her neck. On the way to her funeral, the whole family died when a milk truck plowed into their car on the Staten Island Expressway.

The *Staten Island Advance* splashed the story on its front page, describing the accident scene as "a haunting shade of bright pink"—spilled milk mixing with spilled blood. It also mentioned that the house the family had lived in was bright pink, but it didn't say it was called the Cursed House. The house has been empty ever since.

"Do you really think it's Cursed?" Gayle asks.

"Yeah, it seems like it," I reply.

Gayle stops her spoon in midair. "Do you think it's pink because of blood?"

"Yeah," I say again.

"How come the Curse doesn't come to our house?" she asks, and although she says this nonchalantly, I can tell the idea makes her anxious.

3

I pause, because I really don't know. Finally I say, "I guess Curses don't work that way. I guess Curses just stay where they are."

Gayle nods, satisfied with my response.

Truth is, even though the Cursed House has always been right next door, it isn't a big part of my life and I don't worry about it.

This is a list of the things I *do* worry about:

a. eddie
b. gym
c. my hair
d. being israeli

I make a lot of lists. They help me think. I sometimes write them down, but mostly I just make them in my head.

After eating a second bowl of cereal, I go upstairs to put away my school things. The first thing to greet me when I walk into my room is my poster of Prince Charles and Lady Diana on their wedding day. Gayle bought it for me on my thirteenth birthday. Gayle's birthday—she turned nine—is the day before mine.

"Roxanne!" Gayle suddenly screeches. "Come quick!"

"What? What?" I yell as I run down the stairs.

Gayle is standing in front of the window in our living room, pointing outside, her mouth frozen into a giant O.

A blue station wagon is parked in the driveway of the Cursed House. A woman with a fluffy mound of carrot-orange hair, wearing a brown skirt and yellow jacket, is pulling a sign out of the trunk.

Before I can make out what the sign says, I know what it is. I have seen this exact situation in countless commercials. The woman is a real estate agent, and the sign she slides slowly into place reads:

Sold.

chapter two

it doesn't take long for the news to get around Brookfield Avenue. After being empty for almost a year, the Cursed House was sold again—in just one day!

After the real estate agent with the carrot-orange pompadour drives away, a knot of neighborhood kids gathers around the sign on the lawn of the Cursed House.

Eddie runs his hands over the sign, as if by feeling it he will be able to magically tell us who has been crazy enough to buy the Cursed House. It's not an ugly house, really. Even the bright pink isn't so bad. Except the lawn is kind of gross right now—scattered with old cigarette butts and beer cans.

I stare at Eddie from where Gayle and I stand with our neighbor Kathleen, admiring his white-blond hair and how good his butt looks in his tight jeans. When he turns to look at me, my heart catches in my throat. That always happens when Eddie looks at me. I don't remember exactly when I started liking him. I think I always did. He's so All-American. His gaze rests on me for only a second, though, before searching out Kathleen's face.

"What do you think, Kathleen?" he asks, his blue eyes flashing like a car's high beams.

Kathleen smiles. "You tell me, Eddie," she answers coolly.

I wonder for the hundredth time what he sees in her. Kathleen is the definition of ordinary. There's nothing special about her average face, her average brown hair, her average brown eyes. But Eddie has the biggest crush in the world on her. And the funny thing is, Kathleen likes letting Eddie think he has a chance, but she doesn't give in to him. And this has been going on for five months!

Part of me likes Kathleen and considers her my friend—maybe my only friend, besides Gayle, who doesn't really count. Another part of me wishes she'd disappear. A third part of me has a feeling I hang out with her only because wherever she goes, Eddie goes.

Eddie glances at me. "What do you think?" he asks.

I'm so startled, I feel momentarily numb. I finally manage to mutter, "Uh . . ."

"Uh . . . ," Joe mimics, making a funny face at his friends.

The boys around Joe laugh. I feel my cheeks burn. I have to remind myself that Joe is only eight, even if he is nasty.

"Shut up, Joe," Kathleen snaps.

Joe's gap-toothed grin vanishes immediately, and his friends stop laughing all at once, as if a switch has been turned off. I'm sorry I wished Kathleen would disappear a moment ago.

"Say you're sorry," Kathleen demands.

"Yeah," Eddie joins in. "Say you're sorry." He trudges to where Joe and his little friends stand on the lawn. The boys disperse like cookie crumbs as Eddie towers over them. He grabs Joe by his shirt collar and drags him over to me.

Joe laughs and whimpers at the same time. Eddie shoves Joe toward me—so hard that Joe tumbles to his knees at my feet.

"That's right, on your knees," Eddie says heartily, giving me a wink.

My heart nearly pops out of my chest. This is the most attention Eddie has given me—ever. I smile uncomfortably.

"Say you're sorry," Eddie growls as he stands over Joe.

Joe is crying. I can make out a tiny "Sorry" as it comes out of his mouth. Without any warning, Eddie suddenly brings his fist down, sprawling Joe across the ground. I gaze at Eddie in disbelief.

"Say it louder," he snarls.

"Eddie, stop," Kathleen says, reaching down to help Joe get up. "Are you okay?" she asks him.

Joe sobs and sniffles.

Eddie looks morosely at Kathleen, not sure what to do.

I study the ground, wishing I was the one who had saved Joe, even if it meant yelling at Eddie.

"I'm gonna take Joe home," Kathleen says. She glowers at Eddie, who looks at the ground. Then she walks away, leading Joe by the hand.

I shuffle my feet, not sure what to do now that I'm alone with Eddie. But I don't have to worry about it for long, because a red convertible pulls up in front of the house. It's Margo Defino, who lives in the house on the other side of the Cursed House.

"Wow!" she cries. She hops out of her convertible, whips off her sunglasses, and hurries to the sign. "I don't believe it! It's sold! When did this happen?" she asks, turning in a circle to look at us.

No one answers. Finally Eddie says, "It happened in one day. Today."

"Wow!" she exclaims again, grinning. Then her smile fades. She looks at us curiously. "What are you all doing?" she asks suspiciously. She checks her watch. "It's almost dinnertime. Why don't you all go home?"

Grown-ups don't seem to like seeing a big group of us together. Normally, we'd balk—well, not me, but Eddie or Kathleen would. But this time, in less than a minute, the knot of kids around the Cursed House vanishes into thin air.

chapter three

margo defino told us to go home because of dinnertime, but that's a joke. At our house, anyway.

On *The Brady Bunch*, dinnertime means all six Brady kids, plus Carol and Mike Brady, wolfing down pork chops and applesauce around the dining room table while Alice the housekeeper pours lemonade made from real lemons.

At our house, dinnertime means Gayle and me, alone, with *I Dream of Jeannie* reruns and more Cocoa Pebbles around the kitchen table. Dinnertime is a beautiful concept, but it doesn't work at our house. Not since *Ema*—our mother—left, anyway.

There is one great thing about not having dinner-time. If we were a normal American family, I doubt we'd be allowed to watch TV during dinner. And after *I Dream of Jeannie* ends, my favorite show in the whole world starts.

When the show comes on, Gayle and I sing the theme song at the top of our lungs:

> *Wonder Woman, Wonder Woman.*
> *All the world's waiting for you,*
> *and the power you possess!*
>
> *In your satin tights,*
> *Fighting for your rights*
> *And the old Red, White, and Blue!*

I nearly burst into tears. The song clogs up all the cavities of my chest, making it hard to breathe.

I can't remember much about our naturalization ceremony in Brooklyn the day we became American citizens. I do remember *Ema* crying quietly during the swearing of the oath. I suspect *Ema* felt then what I feel now—positively constipated with red, white, and blue happiness.

I try not to dwell on *Ema*'s absence, because it makes my stomach hurt. I'm glad I have *Wonder Woman* to take my mind off it.

There's something about Wonder Woman—her strength, her beauty, her fabulous hair, her sheer All-Americanness—that makes me yearn to be her. When I was little, all the girls in my class wanted to be Wonder Woman, but I guess I never outgrew it. I mean, wouldn't it be absolutely awesome to fend off bullets with golden bracelets and have a golden lasso that forced people to tell the truth?

When I was nine, I'd twirl around at recess, determined to change into Wonder Woman. That's how Wonder Woman changed from Diana Prince, her real identity, into a superhero. I thought that if I just concentrated on it—*really* concentrated on it—it would work. It didn't, of course, and I gave up. But I still think about it sometimes.

An hour later, *Wonder Woman* is over and we run out of Cocoa Pebbles. Yuck and double yuck. We usually remember we have homework to do around this time, so we take out our schoolbooks and, with the TV still on, work at the kitchen table.

An hour after that, the sky darkens, *Little House on the Prairie* comes on, and we start worrying about *Aba*—our father.

Gayle adores *Little House on the Prairie*, which is about a girl named Laura Ingalls, who has the most wonderful family in the world. Ma and Pa are always there for her—listening, helping, hugging. Ma is the kind of mother who sews lace ruffles onto bonnets, and Pa is the kind of father who teaches Laura Important Life Lessons. They always have dinnertime. They even have breakfast time. They're totally All-American.

At 9:38, Gayle announces she's taking a shower. She says it cheerfully, to hide the fact that she's upset.

By 10:53, we're at the kitchen table, drumming our fingers and not paying attention to *Dynasty*.

I make a decision. "I'm not staying up again," I say to Gayle, my voice shaking. "I'm going to bed."

Gayle yawns. She doesn't reply.

I know most kids love staying up late, but that's because their parents are home. They aren't alone like Gayle and me, worrying, waiting for their father to get home from work.

I trudge up the stairs to my room, getting angrier with each step. By the time I enter my room, I'm seething. I pull off my clothes and throw them in exasperation across the room. I reach behind my pillow for my pajamas with the hole in the seat of the pants and barge into the bathroom.

Why did *Ema* have to leave us? It's been almost three months since she flew to Israel to take care of her sister. We get her letters, but the mail is so slow, and calling is too expensive. My sister and I always fight when we spot that wonderful, flimsy, blue aeromail envelope in our mailbox. We both want to be the first to read it. It's kind of silly to fight over *Ema*'s letters, though, because we both have trouble reading Hebrew—especially when there aren't any vowels.

The Hebrew alphabet is like the English alphabet—there are letters and sounds and all that stuff. But the vowels, instead of being letters like *a, e, i, o, u,* are dots and dashes instead. These dots and dashes go *under* the letters; the letter *gimel,* for instance, which makes a *g* sound, gets its vowel sound from whichever dot or dash is under it. That's how you know to say *goo* or *go* or *guh* or *gah* or *gee.* It's kind of cool and really pretty easy—but when the vowels are missing, it can be very hard. Advanced writing, like in books and newspapers in Israel, usually doesn't have vowels.

Ema used vowels in her letters at first. I guess she was imagining Gayle and me reading them—knowing we'd have trouble if they weren't there. But after a few weeks, the vowels would be in the first few paragraphs of her letter but not the rest of it. And lately, her letters didn't have any vowels at all.

It's like she's forgetting us. Forgetting that Gayle and I are here, waiting and reading. This thought hurts.

I finish in the bathroom. The TV is on in my parents' bedroom, which means Gayle has moved there from the kitchen. I walk down the hall. Gayle is lying in our parents' bed in her pajamas, waiting for *The Tonight Show* so she can pretend to watch it.

"I'm going to sleep," I announce.

"Aren't you worried?" she asks, keeping her eyes on the TV.

"No," I lie.

"Liar," she says, still not looking at me.

I slip back to my room. Falling asleep in my parents' bed in front of the TV is the way Gayle deals. It's the way we both did once. I used to lie there next to her, listening to Johnny Carson's jokes without getting them, panicking, certain that *Aba* was murdered, lying in a pool of his own hot blood in a dark alley. Gayle always fell asleep while I lay awake, waiting, worrying, imagining that murder scene over and over in my mind until it felt so real to me, I swear I could taste *Aba's* blood on my tongue.

For three months it's been like that.

Well, no more.

I'm not going to lie awake anymore.

I'm not going to panic anymore.

I'm not going to wait up for *Aba* anymore.

I'm not going to imagine that hot pool of blood in my mind anymore.

I slide into bed. The sheets are cold, and I curl up into a ball, shivering. The blue-green digits on my clock blink relentlessly at me: "11:39." I turn over onto my stomach and force myself to shut my eyes. But I'm not sleepy.

At 11:53, I can still hear the soft sounds of the TV. I turn over onto my side and face the wall.

At 12:28, I start counting sheep. It doesn't work. Who was the idiot who came up with that stupid idea? And why is it sheep anyway? Why isn't it apple pies or baseballs or cheeseburgers?

At 12:49, a key jingles in the front door.

"*Aba!*" I hear Gayle shout; then comes the sound of her bounding down the stairs.

"*Motek!*" I hear *Aba* cry. *Motek* means "sweetheart" in Hebrew.

I pull the covers over my head.

Now the conversation in the kitchen is growing animated. I pick up words—"Cursed House," "sold in one day," "new neighbors." I turn over twice, but it's useless. Sighing, I pull myself out of bed and head downstairs.

The light in the kitchen is brighter than I expect. I stand in the doorway, squinting and feeling self-conscious in my flimsy pajamas. *Aba* looks up and says, "*Motek*, you were sleeping?"

"No," Gayle answers with a smile. "Roxanne was pretending."

"No, I wasn't," I protest.

Aba motions for me to join him and Gayle at the kitchen table. As usual, he's made peppermint tea. Steam curls out of the three mugs on the table. Three mugs—one for me, too.

I sigh again. "*Aba*, I'm sick of this," I say. My throat tightens, but I ignore it and go on. "Why did she have to leave? When is she coming back?"

Gayle stares alertly at our father. We've asked him this question a hundred times, but he's never really given us an answer.

"Soon," he says. "Very soon."

You'd think we'd press him further on this, but we've done that, and it's never gotten us anywhere.

"Family is important," he says quietly.

That gets me. "But we're her family, too," I say. "What about *us*?"

Aba looks down into his mug. He doesn't answer my question. "She will come home soon," he says.

We're quiet for a few seconds. I take a sip of my tea. I want to cry, but at the same time, I want to be strong. Being strong stinks.

"Can you . . . read her letter again?" Gayle asks.

Every night, Gayle asks *Aba* to read *Ema*'s last letter. This latest one we got seven days ago, without vowels. *Aba* reaches into his back pocket. It occurs to me he probably keeps the letter with him all the time. Does he read it when he's taking a break? Does he study it when he's lined up with all the other taxis in front of Penn Station?

"I miss you all so much," *Aba* reads out loud in Hebrew. "I think about you every minute of every day. I'm sorry you're not happy about the food. I promise that when I come back, we'll have a feast. I promise. I'll be back soon. Very soon."

Even *Ema* won't answer the question.

chapter four

gym is the worst idea ever invented.

Congress should ban it.

I wish someone would blow up the gym and get it over with.

It's the only class where my hands sweat. If gym didn't exist, I wouldn't know hands *could* sweat. It's like those sweat glands are marked *For Gym Use Only*.

I haven't slept well, and the next morning, the last thing I want to think about is the twice-a-week torture known as gym. I've had strange dreams all night involving my mother, murderous Hebrew vowels, and mugs of scalding peppermint tea.

But I do have to think about gym. I have to make sure I wear hole-free panties and my nicest bra. As I wriggle into a satiny white bra, I'm reminded once again of how much I

a. pray for a crazed wacko to set off explosives in the gym
b. wish i could turn into wonder woman
c. long to have my hair work

If I were my sister's age, the hair issue would be nonexistent. I would wear it straight with bangs like Gayle does and be done with it, and nobody would think anything.

But I'm in eighth grade, and in eighth grade you need wings. The hair on each side of your face has to be meticulously rolled into feathery snake-curls, and these curls have to last perfectly all day long. Since I can't make my hair do that, I pull it back with brown barrettes and pretend I have a reason for being the most uncool person in school.

After homeroom, my hands begin their steady spiral toward cold clamminess as I head to gym. I file into the girls' locker room for the ritual Undressing. My hands are slippery as I claw my way out of my clothes. I can't tell you how barbarian it is to throw a bunch of girls together into a room and force them to take off their clothes in front of each other. It has taught me, though, to be the fastest changer on earth. In five seconds flat, I'm in my sweat suit.

Most girls change into shorts, but I need the physical and emotional protection of baggy sweatpants. Once we're all changed, our Too-Chirpy Gym Teacher informs us we're playing indoor Wiffle ball. My stomach plunges eighteen stories. Indoor Wiffle ball is as ferocious and bewildering as any civilized sport can be. The Wiffle ball constantly ricochets off everything in the gym, hurtling unpredictably in all directions, so you never know when it's going to smash into your nose.

Being outside for softball instead of inside for Wiffle ball is semi-decent, because you can hide in the outfield. If you're lucky, you might spend the entire period milling around without having to play at all. Sometimes a ball will come at you, causing a momentary crisis, but nobody is that good in eighth grade. You can miss it without suffering horrible consequences. Besides, I always make sure to stand really far back in the outfield.

See, all balls seem as hard as rocks to me. I always duck when they come toward me instead of trying to catch them. It's a reflex I can't change. I know being good at sports is one of the requirements of being American. But I can't transcend my spazzness, and this is a constant source of humiliation for me.

Our Too-Chirpy Gym Teacher picks two captains and tells them to choose players for their teams. I can't imagine a worse way to do this. My classmates are picked off until it's only me, Gheeta, and Suri. Gheeta and Suri can barely speak English and look strange and smell funny. Why am I in their category?

a. because i'm a spazz?
b. because i'm a fake american, too?

I hear my name called and feel a rush of euphoria. I'm picked before Gheeta and Suri! With a grin, I join my team.

"What are you so happy about?" Donna growls at me.

The grin quickly disappears from my face.

Donna is the scariest person I know. She lives around the corner from us. She smokes, dates boys who are older than her, has perfect wings and makeup, and is fantastic at sports. Her gym clothes—tight blue shorts and tight white top—provide a fascinating show for the boys on the other side of the gym. Whenever she moves, part of her butt peeks out of her shorts.

I wish I had one iota of the Americanness Donna possesses. I take a step away from her, and she turns back to her friends.

As predicted, indoor Wiffle ball is a nightmare. The deafening echo of the ball combined with the loud screech of sneakers on the wooden floor makes me totally paranoid. But the ball never comes near me, so I don't have to catch it, and the class ends before it's my turn to hit. I'm safe again till next time.

The rest of the day is okay. When I get home, I choose a can of sliced mushrooms from the kitchen cupboard. I'm opening it when Gayle gets home.

"Hello," she says cheerily, taking off her backpack. She studies my can of mushrooms. "We're out of cereal?"

"Yup," I say.

Gayle opens the fridge.

"There's no yogurt either," I say, as I fork mushrooms into my mouth. "I'll split this with you."

Gayle frowns. Then her face lights up. "Let's get hot dogs from Kathleen," she says excitedly.

Since *Ema* left, food has become a never-ending source of

a. distress
b. aggravation
c. starvation
d. extinction

Aba's idea of eating is a kitchen cupboard filled with nasty cans of "ethnic food" from a grocery store on the Lower East Side, though there are occasional treasures such as mushrooms. And he can't cook anything except *hijeh*, a kind of Israeli omelet with vegetables.

Gayle and I have resorted to buying food from Kathleen. It's pathetic, I know, but it beats scavenging in garbage cans like a couple of homeless people.

Gayle opens her backpack and pulls out a little gold purse. "I've got two dollars," she says brightly. "That should be enough for four hot dogs."

We walk to Kathleen's house, which is next door to Margo's. We pass the Cursed House on the way. It looks the same. I can't believe some very unlucky human beings are going to move into it.

"I wonder how long before the new people move in," Gayle says, echoing my thoughts.

"Soon, I guess," I say.

"I wonder . . ." Gayle begins but stops.

I know what she's thinking: *I wonder what terrible things will happen to them.*

When we reach Kathleen's house, we see her brothers and sisters throwing a red Frisbee on their front lawn. Kathleen's front lawn isn't really a lawn.

The grass is trampled away because her family is always using it to play sports.

Kathleen's family is super-athletic, super-Irish, and super-American—like the Kennedys, really. My family doesn't even own a Frisbee. Kathleen has so many brothers and sisters, I can hardly keep track of everybody. Her house bustles with constant comings and goings. It's lively and full and fun—it reminds me of *The Brady Bunch*. It never feels lonely or empty or food-extinct.

Kathleen and Eddie are sitting on her front stoop next to her oldest brother, Glenn—who is usually mean and is always red-bumped-pimply-faced—all watching the Frisbee game. My heart begins to thump loudly. I don't want this stupid hot dog exchange to take place in front of Eddie.

But when Kathleen sees Gayle and me, she gets up and walks over, leaving Eddie on the stoop. Eddie seems unhappy about it. I guess he can't stand being away from the love of his life for even one minute. Glenn must notice this, because he suddenly punches Eddie in the arm.

"Eddie has a girlfriend," he says in a singsong voice.

"Shut up," Eddie says, getting up.

We leave them and follow Kathleen into the house, right to the kitchen, where Kathleen's mother is feeding Mikey. Mikey's gurgling in his high chair, his little face smeared with mushy green peas.

"Hi there, girls," Kathleen's mother says pleasantly.

"Do we have hot dogs, Mom?" Kathleen asks.

"Behind the American cheese," Kathleen's mother answers.

Kathleen opens the fridge and moves food around. "I don't see them," she calls over her shoulder.

Kathleen's mother shuts her eyes as if in deep thought. "Check behind the cupcakes. No, the chocolate milk."

Mikey knocks a bag of potato chips to the kitchen floor. Ruffled yellow chips scatter everywhere.

"Oh, Mikey!" Kathleen groans.

"It's all right," Kathleen's mother soothes. "There's a bag of Doritos in the cupboard."

I can hardly contain myself. I exchange a quick glance with Gayle, lick my lips, and ravenously eye the crumbly trail of potato chips on Kathleen's kitchen floor. Hot dogs, American cheese, cupcakes, chocolate milk, potato chips, Doritos. These are the kinds of foods that are missing from our house—delicious American junk foods. *Ema* and *Aba* can't even pronounce Doritos, much less know what they are or understand their importance.

Kathleen finally finds the hot dogs. She wraps four of them in foil.

When we get back outside, Margo Defino is stepping out of her house in a tight red dress and red high heels. Her boyfriend, a crater-faced guy whose name I can never remember, slips an arm around her waist as they walk to his car. When Margo sees us, she waves.

"Where are you going?" Kathleen shouts.

Margo stops and yells back, "The city for dinner and dancing." She shakes her hips.

We all watch as Crater Face opens the car door for her, helps her inside, and goes around to his side of the car. Margo waves one more time before they drive away.

Eddie comes over to stand next to Kathleen. Kathleen eyes him with newfound interest.

I feel suddenly and totally morose. Margo has a boy-friend who takes her to the city for dinner and dancing. Kathleen has Eddie, a mom at home, Doritos, cupcakes, an older-brother bodyguard, and plenty of other siblings to fill her house with activity.

I look down sadly at the package of hot dogs in my hand. If you'd asked me right then and there whether I'd ever

a. feel okay about my hair
b. accept gym
c. watch less tv
d. stop missing my mother

I would have said no.

chapter five

on saturday mornings, Gayle and I get up early to watch cartoons. Yeah, I know—this is little kids' turf. I should be sleeping late on Saturday mornings. I should be in bed till noon. But I get bored just lying around. Besides, one of my favorite shows is on Saturday mornings.

Super Friends is about all the great American superheroes—Superman, Batman and Robin, Wonder Woman, Aquaman, and the Wonder Twins—living together in a place called the Hall of Justice and fighting crime together.

The Wonder Twins are purplish and have weird, pointy faces. They morph into things. Usually, they touch their fists together and say, "Wonder Twin Powers, activate!" Then Jayna, the girl twin, says, "Shape of a gorilla!"—she always seems to choose apes—and Zan, the boy twin, says, "Form of water!" He always seems to end up being carried around in a bucket, but sometimes he turns into something useful, like an ice rocket.

Aba always gets up after *Super Friends* ends. Since Saturday is the busiest night in the city, when almost everyone needs a taxi, he starts working in the afternoon. He usually doesn't get home till the next morning. He shuffles into the kitchen as Gayle and I are watching *The Smurfs*.

He blinks at the TV. "What's that?" he asks with distaste.

"*Smurfs*," Gayle answers merrily. "La-LA-lala-la-LA," she sings.

"Hah?" *Aba* asks.

"That's the theme song," Gayle explains. "La-LA-lala-la-LA."

"Team song?"

"Theme," Gayle repeats. "Th-eme."

"Team," *Aba* says.

"No, not *t. Th.*"

My father tries to pronounce the word again but can't. All Israelis seem to have trouble with *th.*

"I guess I no say it," *Aba* says.

"I guess I can't say it," I correct. It's always been my job to correct my parents' English.

"I guess I can't say it," he repeats, then asks, "Ready soon?"

"Where are we going?" I ask.

"The mall," *Aba* answers definitively, as if there is no other destination on Earth worth considering.

"I want my own *moussaka* this time," Gayle says.

"Okay, okay," *Aba* says with amusement. He turns to me. "You want your own *moussaka* too?"

"I guess," I reply.

Sometimes I wonder what American families do on Saturdays. I'm sure they do more interesting things than what we do. I'm sure they do American things like bowling, or roller-skating, or swimming, or going to the movies, or going on a picnic.

We go to the Staten Island Mall.

Shopping at a mall is a very American thing, but not like we do it. If we were doing it the right way, *Ema* would take us, and actually buy us things, and treat us to lunch at the restaurant inside Macy's, where I would order a strawberry sundae with whipped cream. You can't get more American than that. I bet Donna and her mom do it all the time.

But *Aba* has a whole different routine. First, we go to Sears to browse in the hardware department—fun for him, torture for us. Then we go to the food court for Greek food—the closest we can get to Israeli food. After we eat, *Aba* looks at tires or something equally boring, while Gayle and I pine for designer jeans like the kind Donna wears from Merry-Go-Round or The Limited. Sometimes we play in the arcade.

Nothing special happens with *Aba*'s mall routine today, except that Gayle beats me twice at *Donkey Kong*. When we get back home, a white truck is sitting in the driveway of the Cursed House. It looks like a moving truck. Two red-faced men are closing the back with a loud rumble.

"The new neighbors!" Gayle exclaims.

I'm not the kind of person who can just go up to total strangers, but Gayle jumps out of the car and races up to the men.

"Are you them?" she asks brightly.

The men eye each other in confusion. "What, hon'?" one asks.

"Are you the new neighbors?" she asks, jumping up and down.

The man chuckles. "No, hon'. We're the movers."

"Oh," Gayle says, sounding disappointed. "Then where are they?"

The man checks his watch. "They should be here soon. We just finished moving everything."

Gayle watches as the two men climb into their truck and drive away. The truck belches black smoke as it rounds the corner.

My father gets out of the car. "I get ready for work," he says.

"The new neighbors are going to be here soon," Gayle says excitedly, pointing to the spot where the truck was parked a few seconds ago.

Aba looks over to where Gayle's pointing. "Looks like I miss it," he replies.

I'm about to correct my father's English, but I don't.

It occurs to me that *Ema* and *Aba* miss a lot of important things.

chapter six

after my father leaves for the city, Gayle
and I flip through channels, but Saturday afternoons
are pretty bad TV-wise. There's just too many sports.
This is yet another American thing I'm not good at.
Not only am I terrible at playing sports, but I get bored
watching them, too.

I think about ringing Kathleen's doorbell, but her
family is always busy with something on Saturdays. I
have a ton of homework to do, but the thought of
doing it is unbearable to me. Still, it looks like there

isn't much else going on. I'm about to go up to my room when Gayle yells, "Roxanne! Look!"

She's crouched in front of the living room window. I walk to the window and look out, but Gayle cries, "Get down or they'll see you!"

I lower myself next to her. Like a couple of bank robbers hiding from the police, we peek furtively over the top of the windowsill.

A car is parked in the driveway of the Cursed House. It's the strangest car I've ever seen. It's a station wagon—the kind the Bradys have—but it's covered with pictures. Except for the windshields and windows, not one inch isn't painted with something—and all the pictures seem to be of plants and animals. There doesn't seem to be any organization to it, either. There's an animal that looks like a moose painted next to a cactus, and a palm tree next to a polar bear. The roof has a giant painting of snow-capped mountains.

"Is that an anteater?" I whisper to Gayle, pointing to a picture on the right side of the car.

"Hmmm," Gayle replies. "Maybe an armadillo."

"Right, armadillo," I say, then add, "Maybe you should bring down your animal encyclopedia. It looks like we might need it."

Gayle giggles. "Hey, that looks like an alligator. But why is it next to a penguin?"

"I don't know," I answer. "Maybe it's a riddle."

I hold my breath, waiting for the new neighbors to come out of their freaky car. The first person to get out is the driver. He turns out to be freakier than the car. He has long gray hair pulled back into a ponytail, and he's wearing white pants, a white jacket, and a black shirt open down to his belly button.

"These people are weird," I murmur.

Gayle turns to me. "Well, look where they're living."

The passenger door opens and a girl steps out. A girl that looks about my age. She has thick black hair down to her waist and olive-colored skin. She isn't wearing anything strange, just jeans and a sweatshirt with a picture of a unicorn on it. The man and the girl disappear inside the house. Gayle and I continue staring out the window, but nothing else happens.

"Should we say hello?" Gayle finally asks.

"No," I say quickly. "They probably have a lot of unpacking to do. We shouldn't bother them."

"Yeah," Gayle says sadly. She gazes at their car. "Who painted all those pictures?"

"I dunno," I answer.

Gayle stretches. "Wanna play Legos?"

"No, I've got a lot of homework."

Gayle frowns. "Yeah, me too."

She gives the car one final stare, then goes upstairs. Reluctantly, I follow her.

The new neighbors probably do have a lot of unpacking to do, but that isn't the reason I told Gayle we shouldn't stop by. The very idea of dropping in on them horrifies me. That girl with the black hair and olive skin has to be my age, and

a. what if she doesn't like me?
b. what if she picks on me?
c. what if she's scary like donna?

I'm not going near her. Not ever.

42

I sit at the desk in my room and pull out my schoolbooks. It looks like homework is going to be today's activity. I console myself with the fact that tonight, after all the sports, Gayle and I will watch better TV.

I'm halfway through social studies when I hear a car starting. I peek at the Cursed House from my window. The picture-painted station wagon is pulling away, but the girl isn't in it. The girl's sitting on the front stoop—just sitting there, doing nothing.

I stare at her, trying to decide what kind of girl she is. A few clues are encouraging. For one, she doesn't have wings. This can mean several things:

a. she doesn't know how to make wings, which is good
b. she doesn't care about having them, which is good
c. she's from another country, like gheeta and suri, and doesn't do that sort of thing, which is good

Her jeans aren't tight, and they aren't designer like Jordache, Sasson, or Sergio Valente. This is also good.

She isn't doing anything cruel like squashing ants. More good.

I continue gazing at the girl, wondering what she's like. I get up from my desk and creep silently down the stairs. My only intention is to spy on her from the living room window. But the minute I walk in front of the window, the girl turns around. Her eyes meet mine through the glass.

The girl makes a motion with her hands. A wave. No, a "Come on down" gesture, like from *The Price Is Right*. Well, I can't ignore her now. I take a deep breath and start for the front door. I can still see her through the window as I move toward the door, and, at that moment, the girl blows a huge green bubble that collapses on her face. My hand freezes on the doorknob.

The girl chews gum.

Bad, bad, bad sign.

But the front door opens under my hand, and I find myself standing in the doorway.

"Hi," she says.

"Hi," I reply in a voice that sounds strange to me.

I know she's waiting for me to walk outside and act like a normal person, but I can't make myself take another step.

She reaches into her front pocket. "Want some Bubblicious?" she asks, holding out a packet of green gum. She studies the label. "It's a new flavor—apple. It doesn't taste like a real apple, but it's pretty good."

I don't reply or move, but what she says nearly knocks me over. How many girls would admit to liking apples? How many girls would compare the newest flavor of Bubblicious to real fruit—as if somehow a real apple was better?

I've always wanted to tell people that watermelon-flavored Jolly Ranchers don't taste like real watermelon, but I don't, because they'd think I was a loser for saying such a stupid thing. Before I can stop myself, though, my mouth says, "Jolly Ranchers never taste like their fruit either."

The girl nods. "Especially watermelon," she says.

I want to do a dance. Instead, I walk toward her. The girl holds out the packet of gum to me. I help myself to a piece.

"This is a nice neighborhood," the girl says.

I nearly choke on my Bubblicious.

"The neighborhood we lived in before wasn't this nice," she continues. "But the one before that was really nice."

"How many places have you lived?" I ask, not believing I'm actually having a conversation with this girl, who seemed so terrifying a moment ago.

"A lot of places," she replies. She flips her hair out of her face. It's gorgeous hair, even without the wings.

"What's your name?" I ask.

"Liat."

My eyes widen. "Liat?"

"Yeah. What's yours?"

For a moment, I don't answer. Finally, I reply, "Roxanne."

"That's really nice," she says.

I have a cousin in Israel named Liat. *Ema*'s girlfriend in Brooklyn is named Liat. Liat is an Israeli name.

"My dad's name is Yossi," she goes on.

"You're Israeli!" I blurt out like an idiot.

"Yeah," she says warily.

It occurs to me that she might not understand my reaction. "We're Israeli, too," I say quickly.

"You are?" she asks. "Then why's your name Roxanne?"

I shut my mouth abruptly. This is a subject I carefully avoid.

"I changed it," I say simply.

Usually people ask, "From what?" but Liat just nods.

The front door opens and Gayle flies out. "I heard you," she says to me in a tone that sounds like an accusation.

"What's your name?" Liat asks.

Gayle turns to her. "Gayle."

Liat winks. "Gotcha, *Gayle*."

Gayle gives me a funny look. I feel like I should say something, but at that moment, Joe and his dumb little friends stride up the sidewalk.

"That's Joe," Gayle announces. "He lives down the block."

"Yeah," Joe says in a swaggering tone. "Who're you?"

Liat fixes Joe with a steady gaze. "Liat," she replies coolly.

I can tell Joe doesn't like Liat's tone one bit. "Yeah, well, that's a weird name," he says. "And your house is Cursed. So you better watch out."

"Yeah," some of the other boys echo. "You better watch out."

If I were in this situation, my face would immediately burn red.

But Liat doesn't even blink. Without missing a beat, she says, "No, *you* better watch out. Because if you bother me, I'll put a Curse on you."

chapter seven

gayle and i exchange looks of amazement.

Joe mumbles something about the house being Cursed again and shuffles off with his little friends in tow.

"You showed him," Gayle says proudly.

Liat shrugs. "He's just a little kid."

I frown. Joe is just a little kid. Liat has stated the obvious. And yet I've always been afraid of him because he's so mean. It makes me feel like a moron. Have I been terrified all this time of a peewee?

Liat holds out the green packet of Bubblicious to my sister.

"Ooh, apple," Gayle purrs in pleasure, taking a piece and popping it into her mouth. "My favorite's regular, but grape's good, too."

Now that Joe has stormed off, I think Liat will ask us to explain the Curse.

But she doesn't.

I think she'll ask us which school she'll be going to and what it's like.

But she doesn't.

I think she'll ask us about the other kids on the block and whether they're all nasty like Joe.

But she doesn't.

If I were Liat, those are the questions I would ask. But Liat asks us about our parents.

Yes, our parents.

"What are their names?"

"Ruth and Adam," Gayle replies, her mouth moving in great, slow, chewing motions.

"Biblical names," Liat murmurs. "So, they fit right in, I guess."

I raise my eyebrows. My parents definitely do *not* fit in. "What do you mean?"

"Their names sound like American names," Liat replies. "Because they're from the Bible."

"Oh," I mutter in bewilderment.

"My dad's name is Joseph, which is a biblical name, too," Liat goes on, "but he likes Yossi. So even though it's easier for him to use Joseph, he uses Yossi."

I think about that. Liat's father would rather have a name that's troublesome, because he likes it, than change it. For a moment, I feel guilty.

Liat seems to sense this, because she asks, "Did you get made fun of a lot?"

I study her intently, not sure if I can trust her. Before I can answer, though, Gayle chimes in, "Oh, yeah. Roxanne got made fun of a lot. But not me so much."

I feel my face flame. I want to strangle Gayle. But Liat says in a kind voice, "I understand. Americans don't like anything too strange." She smiles at me. "What was your Israeli name?"

I don't want to say it. I hate saying it. The reason my name is Roxanne is because my old name brought me only pain and suffering.

From the earliest time I can remember, kids called me "rabbit" and "ravioli," and one horrible boy even made up a rhyme that he relentlessly sang to me:

Ra-VEET!
Rah-Vo!
Bah-Ben!
Bah-Boe!

It wasn't so much the lyrics themselves that bothered me—they didn't mean anything, anyway. It was the fact that he was giving me the wrong kind of male attention. Other girls were getting invited to roller-skating parties; I was being musically mortified.

"Ravit," I say in a near-whisper.

"That's pretty," Liat replies.

"Not here," I retort angrily.

Normally, people argue. But Liat only says, "Yeah, you're right. But in Israel it would be beautiful."

Beautiful?

Liat's right. In Israel, *Ravit* would be like *Jennifer* or *Michelle*. A beautiful girl's name.

"How'd you pick Roxanne?" Liat asks.

"Oh, I just kind of liked it," I say.

This is a lie. I've never told anyone the real reason.

I picked it because in fifth grade Roxanne Morrow was the most popular girl in school, inexplicably adored by girls and boys, teachers and lunch ladies, even the janitor. I mistakenly believed that if I called myself Roxanne, too, the glittering sheen of her popularity would magically rub off on me. So when we entered sixth grade in the new middle school, I became Roxanne.

Of course, I was totally wrong.

I never saw Roxanne Morrow again. I think she transferred to Catholic school that year. And nobody teased me—or even noticed—my renaming. I guess having an American name doesn't automatically make you popular.

"What were you?" Liat asks Gayle.

"Gili," she answers.

"That's pretty, too," Liat says.

Gayle beams. Then she asks the question I'm dying to know the answer to. "How come you never changed your name?"

Liat leans back against the stoop. "I guess I didn't want to."

I feel guilty again, and my Bubblicious is losing its flavor. Or maybe it's the lousy taste in my mouth.

Liat asks, "How old were you when you came to America?"

"Five," I reply.

"I was one," Gayle answers excitedly. "I was a baby."

"I was five, too," Liat says, nodding at me. Then she asks, "What do your parents do?"

"*Ema* works at a nursing home," Gayle says. "She wipes old people's butts all day. But she's in Israel now, taking care of her sister. Her sister has cancer." She pauses. "*Aba* drives a taxi in Manhattan. What do your parents do?"

"My father's a painter," Liat replies. "My mom died."

This statement hushes Gayle immediately. I know it's rude to be nosy, but I can't help it. "When?" I ask.

Liat looks me right in the eye. "When I was four. She was killed by a bomb. It exploded in a bus station in Tel Aviv."

I don't know what to say to that, so I say nothing.

We hear a car. The painted station wagon hurries down the street and pulls into the driveway. Liat's father gets out of the driver's side. From the passenger's side, the strangest woman I've ever seen in my whole life steps out.

Her hair is the color of a peeled banana. It's long and frizzy and looks weird against her dark skin. She's wearing a lacy white top that's see-through, and I can make out a tiger-print bra underneath. Her skirt is made of black leather, and she wears it below her belly button, which is outlined in a blue circle.

"*Booba!*" she yells in a high, scratchy voice, running toward us. She throws her arms around Liat, enveloping her in a bear hug. When they finally part, she looks curiously at us. "*Mee zeh?*" she asks, which means "Who is this?" in Hebrew.

Liat is smiling. "This is Rivka. My dad's girlfriend."

I study Rivka. She's a *weirdo*.

"This is Roxanne and Gayle," Liat says. "They live here." She points to our house.

Liat's father walks over to us. He looks even more ridiculous up close.

"You make friends already, eh, *booba*?" he says in a merry voice. *Booba* means "doll."

His accent is thick, much thicker than my parents'. And he's much more clueless about clothing than my parents ever were.

"*Y'alla!*" Rivka exclaims, which means "Let's go!" She places a hand on my shoulder. "We eat."

I glance in confusion at Liat. Rivka says again, "*Y'alla*. You three *boobot*."

Liat grins at us. "Rivka is an awesome cook."

Rivka's hands explode into a frenzy of gestures. "We have feast, eh? *Falafel*, *hummus*, *baba ghanoush*, *tabbouleh*, *borekas*, *kubeh*. *Y'alla*. We eat."

I shrug at Gayle, and we follow them into their house. I'm actually drooling over the possibility of having such a feast.

I almost forget we're entering the Cursed House. We've never been inside it. Gayle suddenly grips my arm.

I look carefully around me, expecting a giant Komodo dragon to tear out of a closet or something. But nothing happens. The house is completely normal. It's mostly empty except for lots of cardboard boxes.

Rivka leads the way into the kitchen, muttering to herself in Hebrew, and pulls pots, pans, bowls, and platters out of boxes. She also takes great quantities of things out of the refrigerator.

In a matter of minutes, Rivka has us working— rolling *falafel* balls, roasting eggplant for the *baba ghanoush*, chopping parsley for the *tabbouleh*, slicing pita bread. It reminds me so much of *Ema*, I feel like I'm in a parallel universe. Gayle and I always helped *Ema* cook—except we asked her to make American foods, like meat loaf and mashed potatoes and pot roast and green bean casserole. Even though I've had these Israeli foods before, I've never actually made them. It feels strange, but in a good way.

It takes almost two hours to get Rivka's Israeli feast ready, but it's fun. It's like a party. It's when I'm popping my fifth *falafel* ball into my mouth that I realize Gayle and I will miss *The Love Boat* on TV if we don't get going soon.

Normally, this would bother me a lot, but today it doesn't.

chapter eight

we see aba the next morning for a little while before he has to leave for work again.

"And we had *beera schora*, too. It was great," Gayle tells him triumphantly.

My sister has just finished describing our feast at Liat's house in all its glory. She seems especially dazzled by the *beera schora*, which means "black beer." Black beer isn't really beer. It's a kind of malted drink Israelis love.

"So, they're nice neighbors," *Aba* says. "They're Israeli."

"Yeah!" Gayle cries excitedly.

"And he paints," *Aba* says.

"Yeah," Gayle replies. "He painted the pictures on their car. But he paints houses to make money."

My dad nods thoughtfully. I wonder if he's dreaming of the latex paint department at Sears. A little later, he leaves for Manhattan.

Gayle goes to the fridge and pulls out the packages of foil-wrapped leftovers Rivka gave us. She spreads them out on the table and unwraps each one, then happily hands me a fork.

"*Be tay ah von*," I say to her, which means "bon appétit." We dig in.

"You know, we forgot about *Love Boat* last night," Gayle says as she stuffs her face full of *baba ghanoush*.

"I know," I say. "But I didn't really miss it. I mean, we still had fun."

"Yeah," Gayle says, her cheeks bloated with food. "That's how I felt, too."

"You know, this tastes even better today than it did yesterday," I say, shoveling a piece of pita bread piled high with *hummus* into my mouth.

"Hey, look," Gayle cries, pointing at a listing in *TV Guide*. "*Grease* is on today."

"It is?" I ask with my mouth full.

Gayle turns to me with her eyes shining. "Wow, this is turning out to be a great day."

Sunday afternoons are usually good days for TV movies, but the movies aren't always as good as *Grease*. Usually they show boring movies like *The Grapes of Wrath* or *Requiem for a Heavyweight*.

It doesn't occur to me to see what Liat's doing today. On Sundays the kids on the block usually go to church or visit relatives. So I'm surprised when our doorbell rings and it's Liat standing on our stoop.

"What're you doing today?" she asks.

"*Grease* is on TV," I squeal.

"So what?" she says. "You wanna do something?"

"But . . . *Grease* is on," I repeat.

Liat looks at me like I'm stupid. "I don't wanna sit home and watch TV. Let's do something."

"Like what?" I shoot back.

"I don't know. What's there to do around here?"

Gayle and I look at each other blankly.

"Well," I venture. "There's town."

"Town?"

"Yeah, it's where all the stores are. By the train station."

"What's in town?"

"Well," I say, "there's a bakery and a pet store."

"And there's banks and dry cleaners and stuff like that, but we don't usually go to those stores," Gayle adds.

"So," Liat says. "*Y'alla.*"

It's the first time Liat has used Hebrew with us, and it feels weird. But it also feels . . . nice.

When neither Gayle nor I move, Liat says, "I guess you don't want to miss *Grease.*" She doesn't say it in a mean way.

"Well," I stall, not wanting to miss *Grease* at all, "do you have . . . any money?"

Liat pulls a bill from her pocket—a twenty.

"Twenty dollars?" I ask. "Where'd you get twenty dollars?"

"Rivka gave it to me," she says. "She said it was a new-house present."

I glance sideways at Gayle. We can't pass up the opportunity to go to town with twenty dollars to spend, even if it does mean missing *Grease.* In ten minutes flat, we're all outside, ready to go.

To get to town, you have to walk past our block to a dead end. At the dead end, there are these ancient, moss-covered stone steps that lead down to a gravel parking lot by the train station. You have to cross a narrow bridge over the train tracks, and then you're in town.

When I was little, I was afraid to cross that bridge. I thought it would collapse under my feet just as a train thundered below me. It still gives me the creeps. I always speed up to get to the other side as quickly as possible.

We start walking to the end of the block. Gayle regales Liat with all the delicious things we can buy at the bakery with her twenty-dollar bill—chocolate éclairs, mile-high napoleons, moist rainbow cookies, fat cream puffs.

"But the spice cakes are the best," Gayle says, smacking her lips.

"Yeah," I agree, nodding my head. "You *have* to try the spice cakes."

I came across a recipe in a magazine at the dentist's office a few years ago for Old-Fashioned Yankee Spiced Cake. It was right around Thanksgiving—for me, the Ultimate All-American Holiday. I love making a big deal out of it. I always help *Ema* make all the traditional American foods. Old-Fashioned Yankee Spiced Cake is a big round cake with a hole in the center of it, drizzled with brown sugar icing. I thought it would be perfect. I mean, it sounded so American, like something the Bradys and Ingalls would serve at Thanksgiving. It even had the word "Yankee" in it!

The recipe for Old-Fashioned Yankee Spiced Cake turned out so well that Thanksgiving that we made it every year from that point on—not just for Thanksgiving but for Rosh Hashanah, too. Rosh Hashanah is the Jewish New Year in the fall, and the menu always includes apples and honey. Old-Fashioned Yankee Spiced Cake doesn't have any apples in it, but it does have honey. It seemed like the perfect dessert to combine being Israeli with being American.

But with *Ema* gone now, we didn't celebrate Rosh Hashanah this year, and we didn't have Old-Fashioned Yankee Spiced Cake. My sister and I discovered spice cakes at the bakery the same week we missed Rosh Hashanah. Discovering them made us feel close to *Ema*—even though the bakery's spice cakes are more like oversized cupcakes with chocolate icing.

We reach the dead end and walk down the moss-covered steps. We make it to the bottom and cross the bridge. Liat stands at the edge of the bridge for a moment, looking down at the train tracks.

"This reminds me of West Virginia," she says. "A lot of trains were always coming through the town we lived in."

"West Virginia?" I ask in astonishment.

"Yeah," Liat replies. "Lots of mountains."

"How come you've lived in so many places?" I ask her, feeling a touch of envy. I've never even been to Pennsylvania, and that's just one state over from New Jersey, which is next door to New York, which is where Staten Island is.

Liat pauses. "We moved to America after my mom died. My dad has this thing about seeing America, so we move around a lot."

"But don't you have to start a new school every time you move? And leave your old friends? And make new friends?" I ask.

Liat shrugs. "Yeah. But it's okay. I'm used to it."

I try to imagine the unspeakable torture of starting

a new school every few years. Just when you figure things out and make friends, it's

ding-dong!
i'm sorry! your time is up!
go back to start!

Every few years it's

go back to start!
go back to start!
go back to start!

We arrive at the bakery, and Liat buys spice cakes, cream puffs, linzer tarts, cream-cheese brownies, napoleons, and chocolate éclairs. We stuff ourselves while watching fuzzy yellow puppies play in the pet store window. By the time we get home, our fingers and mouths are sticky with sweetness. We sit on our stoop and continue gorging ourselves until I start to feel sick.

I'm finishing a chocolate éclair that's leaking milky filling all over my fingers when I spot Kathleen and

Glenn. They're walking toward us in their church clothes, he in beige pants and a striped shirt, she in a white dress with ruffles the color of Creamsicles. Even in nice clothes, Glenn always manages to look red-bumped-pimply-faced and mean.

Whenever I see Kathleen on Sundays wearing her pretty church dresses, I wish I did that too. My parents have American Jewish friends who go to synagogue, but Israelis don't usually go, except maybe during the High Holy Days—the holidays around Rosh Hashanah. Most Israelis aren't religious. When you live in Israel, I guess you don't need to go to synagogue to feel Jewish.

Kathleen once asked us why we didn't go to church. First I had to explain we were Jewish. Then I had to explain we were Israeli. Then I had to explain the difference between the two. I still don't think she understands.

"Hi," she says tentatively.

"Oh, hi," I say, my mouth bloated with cream. I point to Liat. "That's Liat. She moved in yesterday."

"Liat?" Kathleen asks curiously.

"Yeah," Liat replies, but not defensively. "What are your names?"

"Kathleen and Glenn."

"Want éclairs?"

"Sure."

Kathleen and Glenn each accept a leaky éclair. They lick the oozing cream before taking big chomps. More cream splatters out. They hurriedly lick it clean again.

"We had spice cakes, too," Gayle says as she licks each of her fingers.

"This is good," Kathleen says.

"Where'd you move from?" Glenn asks.

"Ohio," Liat says.

"She's lived in West Virginia too," Gayle adds.

Glenn shrugs. "We went to Florida last year," he says.

"We lived there, too," Liat says, licking chocolate icing off her éclair.

"Really? How many places have you lived?" Kathleen asks.

"Lots."

"Where?"

"Alaska."

"Alaska?!"

"Vermont, California, Texas."

"Wow."

Liat smiles. "My dad paints pictures on the car to remind us of places we've lived."

I think of the polar bear next to the alligator next to the armadillo. Now it makes sense. I wonder what Liat's father will paint to remind them of this place. Rats, probably. Or a smelly landfill.

Eddie jogs over from across the street, wearing gray pants and a blue shirt—his church clothes. The blue shirt matches his eyes exactly. That familiar pounding begins in my heart.

"Hey," he says, stopping just short of the stoop and giving Glenn a cool look. "Are you the new girl?"

Liat nods and rescues a blob of cream from plopping onto her jeans.

"So, anything happen yet?"

Liat gives him a puzzled look. Before she can respond, Eddie goes on, "Anyone die yet?"

"Eddie!" Kathleen cries.

"What?" he asks indignantly. "I just wanna know." He turns back to Liat. "Anyone fall down the stairs or anything? Break their neck or anything?"

"Eddie!" Kathleen says again, and Liat asks, "What are you talking about?"

"Didn't anyone tell you?" Eddie asks with a grin, clearly enjoying himself. "About the Curse?"

"Oh, yeah, the Curse," Liat says knowingly. I turn to her, wondering if she really knows or is just pretending to know. Joe stormed off that time before explaining it in all its gory detail, and I've never brought it up.

"Oh, so you know? About how people died and stuff? Are you scared?" Eddie asks eagerly.

"No, I'm not scared," Liat replies evenly.

"Well, you should be," Eddie says, sounding a bit like Joe and his dumb friends. " 'Cause you're gonna die soon."

"Eddie!" Kathleen yells for the third time. "Stop being a jerk!"

"No, it's okay," Liat says. "I'm not afraid of anything." She leans forward. "Or anyone."

Maybe it's Liat's jet-black hair or the sheer audacity in her voice. But I get a severe case of goose bumps all of a sudden—like I've just caught a glimpse of Wonder Woman passing through or something.

chapter nine

liat's father decides that Liat should be in my class at school.

It bugs me royally. I don't want Liat to know what a social loser I am. It's much safer to just live next door to her and occasionally go to town for spice cakes. What if she gets all popular and ends up ganging up on me with Donna and her friends?

My school has ten eighth-grade tracks, and you don't pick the one you want to be in, but Liat's father is determined. He puts on another weird outfit and drives us to school on Monday morning.

If I were starting a new school, I'd be

a. chewing off my fingernails
b. freaking out
c. sweating bullets as big as beach
   balls from my super-reliable
   hand glands

But Liat isn't doing any of these things. She's sitting in the backseat looking calmly out the window as if we're on our way to the mall.

"Are you nervous?" I ask.

She turns to me. "Not really. Are you?"

"Why should I be nervous?" I ask huffily.

Liat gives me a knowing look but says nothing.

"Even if they put you in the same homeroom as me, we switch classes, like, every period," I say. Liat still says nothing, so I go on, "They'd have to, like, *stick* you to me personally, if they wanted you to be in every class with me." Her continued silence only makes me babble onward. "Like, some of us take algebra and some of us take regular math." I want to shut up, but I can't. "Or some of us have U.S. History and some of us have Western Civ."

"I know, Roxanne," she finally says. "It's like that at other schools, too."

"I'm just saying, that's all."

"It'll be fine. Don't worry so much."

"I'm not worried," I say, irritated.

That knowing look again.

I study what she's wearing. It doesn't scream

step right up and see the geek!

But it isn't cool either. Her jeans are faded and her sweatshirt's worn.

"All the girls here have wings," I say. "The cool girls." I realize I've just admitted I'm not one of them. It's not like Liat wouldn't have found out the truth the minute we got to school, but it's too bad I've been uncool for so long that I can't even pretend it for the five-minute drive.

"How come you don't have wings?" I ask.

"It takes too much time."

"Do you know how to make them?"

"Yeah, Rivka showed me. She works in a beauty salon."

I try to imagine Rivka in a work environment. I wonder how she dresses. "Maybe you could show me," I venture.

Liat smiles. "Sure. But it takes a lot of time. I think your hair is fine."

I snort. "My hair is very uncool." There. I admitted it. Again.

"Why do you worry so much about being cool?"

"I don't worry about it," I reply, looking away.

So maybe I *do* worry about it. A lot. But I don't feel like discussing it with Liat. Right now, especially. Or maybe ever.

We arrive at P.S. 32. Liat's father parks his freaky station wagon in the school parking lot. Thank goodness the parking lot is *behind* the school. Since most kids walk to school, everyone is gathered at the front door. The pictures on the car are nice and all, but they wouldn't draw the kind of attention Liat needs right now. Or I need.

We walk into the building and make our way down the hall to the main office. Inside is a high counter manned by a silver-haired mutant whose mouth cannot form what is generally accepted as a smile. When she lays her watery gray eyes on Liat's father, though, they grow as round as golf balls.

"I need a favor," he says smoothly, placing his hands on the counter.

"A favor?" Silver-Haired Mutant asks in disgust, drawing back.

"Yes, a favor, miss," he says, smiling. He turns to Liat. "This is my daughter." He tenderly strokes her cheek. "This is her first day of school." He turns to me. "This is her new friend. She lives next door to us. She is wonderful girl."

My face burns. This is about as embarrassing as parental behavior can get.

"It would make all of us so happy if two girls could be in same class," he says. "Do you think you could find in your heart to help us? It mean so much to us." I wonder what she makes of his broken English.

"Your name?" Silver-Haired Mutant asks me.

I'm startled. It takes me a few seconds to remember it. "Roxanne Ben-Ari," I finally whisper.

"Your daughter's name?"

"Liat Asher," Liat's father answers solemnly.

Without a word, Silver-Haired Mutant leaves the counter and vanishes into another room. We wait, me dying quietly of suspense and embarrassment, wondering what on Earth is happening.

Silver-Haired Mutant returns, holding two manila folders—one for each of us, I suppose. "SPE-10," she says, making a notation in each folder. "You were tracked to that from the beginning, except for gym, when we got the records from your previous school. But I'll make sure your class schedules are exactly the same."

"Thank you so very, very much," Liat's father says. "You are so, so kind." He pats her hand. She smiles at him.

I can't believe any of this:

a. silver-haired mutant exercised her smile muscles for the first time in history?

b. **liat was tracked to my class from the beginning?**

c. **except for gym, my most hated torture?!**

"Okay, my sweet girls," Liat's father says as we leave the office. "You have a great day." He takes Liat into his arms, then gives me a stifling hug. I'm not expecting it and stiffen in his arms. "Take good care of each other." He walks away, stopping to blow us a kiss, and disappears around a corner. I watch him go, trying to make sense of these astounding events.

"Well," Liat says breezily, disrupting my thoughts, "where to?"

I turn to her, my face grim. "Homeroom," I reply. "Then gym."

Nothing like a trial by fire.

≈ ≈ ≈

Homeroom is in a music classroom. The desks are arranged on levels. The cool kids sit in the back. Nerds sit up front. Liat and I sit right in front of the teacher's desk. The Nerd District.

The first-period bell rings shortly after we take our seats, because we've missed most of homeroom visiting Silver-Haired Mutant. Everyone rises and heads for the door. We make our way through the halls to gym. As always, my hands begin to drip salt water. By the time we enter the locker room, they're practically snow cones.

Our Too-Chirpy Gym Teacher gives Liat a locker next to mine. I don't know if I'm surprised or not when I notice Liat doesn't seem to mind the Undressing. I pull off my regular clothes only when I'm ready to pull on my gym clothes at exactly the same moment. It's a system I've perfected for maximum protection. But like many of the other girls in the locker room, Liat strips down to her bra and panties, then leisurely looks around for her gym clothes.

When we're all dressed for our twice-a-week torture, our Too-Chirpy Gym Teacher informs us we're playing softball outside today. I want to jump for joy. The teacher selects two captains.

It's not me, Gheeta, or Suri. It never is. I am a First-Class Nerd of the Sacred Order, unworthy of sports, un-American, uncool. I didn't want Liat to know any of this.

Our classmates are picked off until it's me, Liat, Gheeta, and Suri. I wonder what Liat makes of this humiliating savagery. She must have taken gym at other schools. For the first time, I wonder how schools in other states handle gym. Is gym like this in Alaska? I picture people dogsledding to school in heavy fur coats and conducting the Undressing in an icy igloo.

Liat is picked last.

I glance at her to see how she feels about it, but her face is expressionless.

Our team heads outside.

"Do you know how to play softball?" I ask her in a low voice.

"Sure," she answers.

Donna, who is walking ahead of us in her butt-peeking-out-for-boys shorts, spins around. "Oh, you do, do you?" she asks viciously. She has impossibly long eyelashes—evidence of total mastery in mascara application. "Let's make you first baseman, then. See how you do."

I want to kill myself. Why did I ask Liat that question? Now look what I've done!

Liat places a hand on my shoulder as we reach the field. I nearly yelp. I wasn't expecting her to touch me.

"It's cool," she says with a small smile.

I don't know what to say in response, so I just jog to my outpost at the far end of the field.

The game begins. As usual, few balls come to the outfield, which is exactly the way I like it. Halfway through the game, a ball whizzes toward Liat. I want to shut my eyes, but I force myself to keep them open.

Liat catches it in her mitt.

On the fly.

I rub my eyes in disbelief.

Liat's catch is the third out. Our team exchanges places with the other team. I position myself last in line. If it's timed right, gym will end before I have to hit the ball.

Donna suddenly appears. "You're up," she says
to Liat.

Liat walks to the plate. She picks up the bat. She
looks comfortable. When the ball comes, she whacks it
hard and sends it right over the pitcher's head and past
the outfielders.

Am I dreaming?

Liat navigates the bases. When she returns to home
plate, Donna raises her palm.

Liat high-fives it.

chapter ten

"it didn't mean anything, roxanne."

"It did too, Liat."

"I'm the one who did it."

"But I saw it!"

Liat and I have been sitting on her stoop arguing about her home-run-and-high-five for so long, I've missed *Gilligan's Island*. If I don't get my carcass in the house soon, I'll miss *Wonder Woman*.

"What you did meant something," I say.

"Not if I didn't want it to mean anything," Liat replies.

I'm not saying what I'm really thinking. The truth is, Liat can be good at sports, even if it's the most All-

American sport of them all. And she can high-five any-body she wants. And be friends with anybody she wants.

What I'm really thinking is

why can't it be me?

"Why didn't you tell me?" I mutter.

I don't know if Liat understands what I'm getting at. But she does, because she says, "I didn't know gym was so important to you. I didn't think it was a big deal."

"It's a *huge* deal," I say bitterly.

"Why?"

That stops me.

Because:

a. being brilliant at sports makes you cool and popular
b. and therefore makes you all-american
c. i am not brilliant at sports
d. i am not cool and popular
e. i am not all-american
f. i will never be all-american

"Look," I say, standing up. "I'm going to miss my shows."

Liat seems puzzled. "Shows?"

I clear my throat. "Yeah, you know, TV shows."

Liat frowns at me. "Come on, Roxanne, let's keep talking about this."

"But I can't miss *Wonder Woman*." This sounds lame and is lame, but it's the truth, and besides, I've had enough.

"Why do you have to watch *Wonder Woman*?" Liat asks.

That stops me, too.

Because:

a. wonder woman is all-american
b. liat pulled a wonder woman move today
c. i will never be like wonder woman— or like liat

But I can't say this to Liat. And I can't tell her my biggest fear—that any second now I'll say something moronic . . . and she won't like me anymore.

I start to move toward the door. At that moment, Joe struts up the walk with his never-far-behind-him troop of little boys in tow.

"Oh, what do you want now?" I ask, then gape at my own outburst.

Joe seems shocked. But he recovers quickly.

"You've got food on your face," he says to Liat, which is true. Liat has a tiny speck of pink bubble gum stuck to her upper lip.

Liat automatically brings a hand to her mouth but says nothing in response. I can't tell if she's embarrassed about it.

"Oh, leave her alone," I say, surprising myself again. But I take a deep breath and go on. "If you came here to annoy us, you're wasting your time."

I head into the house, leaving Joe and Company in my dust, stunned at my own boldness.

chapter eleven

saturday morning.

Super Friends.

Wondering if I will ever hit a home run in my entire life. Wishing I could turn into Wonder Woman, marry Superman, and live in the Hall of Justice happily ever after.

Gayle and I are on our second bowls of Captain Crunch when the doorbell rings. It's Liat.

"Whatcha doing today?" she asks brightly.

Gayle and I look at each other. "Nothing," I reply.

I had assumed Liat was a regular kind of person, the kind who holds grudges, like Kathleen. But she's forgotten our little argument from the other day as if it never happened. And don't look at me, because I'm not about to bring it up again.

"Want to do something?" Liat asks.

Pause. "Well," I try to explain, "my dad usually takes us to the mall."

"Want to come with us?" Gayle asks.

"Sure."

I want to kill Gayle. I don't want Liat there. It will be too weird.

An hour later, the four of us are wandering around Sears.

"This is the boring part," Gayle explains.

Aba is in his glory—surrounded by hammers and saws and screwdrivers and tubes of caulk. I wonder why the world needs robin's-egg-blue caulk. *Aba* carefully examines fifty boxes of nails before choosing one. He pays for it, and we're off to the food court.

It takes a few minutes, but we finally find a free table. The family that used it before us made an ugly mess. There's a puddle of soda on the floor and soaked napkins disintegrating in a disgusting mountain on top of the table.

"*Chazeerim*," says Liat, which is exactly what I think—pigs.

Liat and Gayle go to the Greek stand to get the food while I sit silently with *Aba*. At the table next to us, a toddler is holding a mustard-drenched hot dog in each hand without buns. He's waving them in jagged circles and mustard is splattering everywhere. His mother ignores him. I turn to *Aba*. Something's been bugging me, but I hesitate.

"How come you never talk about anything, *Aba*?" I ask before I lose my nerve. Is it an Israeli gene—this not bringing up things? Liat and *Aba* both clearly possess it. "How come you never answer my question about when *Ema*'s coming back?"

Aba turns to me. He seems bewildered. "I don't know," he says. He's silent again.

I frown. This isn't going the way I want it to go.

"You want to talk?" he asks.

"No," I snap.

"Okay," he says.

I sit there fuming. It's absurd! My father asking me if I want to talk, as if he's Mike Brady or Pa Ingalls, pretending to care. I turn to him again. "How come you never, like, pursue anything?"

"Pursue?" he asks.

"Yeah, ask me more than once about something."

Aba shrugs. "Asking once is enough," he says.

"It's not enough," I say.

"How much is enough?"

I can't believe this. "Three times," I sputter, as if I've had this answer prepared the whole day. "Three times is enough."

"Okay," he says, then asks me three times in a row, "Are you going to talk to me? Are you going to talk to me? Are you going to talk to me?"

"No, no, no," I say.

"Okay," he says with another shrug.

I don't know if this lack of communication is an Israeli thing or an *Aba* thing, but either way, I don't like it.

Gayle and Liat return with the food. We eat in silence. I can hardly taste my *moussaka*. See, the thing is, Carol Brady would never fly off to another country and leave her family for three months. Maybe that's something Israelis do, but Americans don't do that to their kids.

After we're done eating, *Aba* says he needs to look at car batteries in the Auto Center. He says he'll meet us at the arcade.

We take the escalator down to the first floor. The arcade is packed. Bleeping, whirring, and shooting noises drift out. There are four guys blocking the entrance. They look like thugs. They have ornate green tattoos all over their arms and spiked blue hair.

I hesitate. So does Gayle. Liat does, too. Finally, she walks over.

"Um, excuse me," she says to the tallest thug.

"Oh, sorry," he says, jumping out of her way.

My jaw falls open. Gayle and I follow Liat inside.

We head to the *Ms. Pac-Man* machine and plug in two quarters.

"Weren't you afraid of those guys?" I ask Liat.

"What could they do to me?" she says. Liat is pretty good at *Ms. Pac-Man*. She gets all the way to the third level on her first life. I guess they have arcades in West Virginia and Texas and Alaska.

"I don't know," I say. "Punch you in the stomach."

"All I said was 'excuse me.' They were blocking the entrance."

"I know, but . . ."

"But what?" Liat turns to me. Pinky just ate her Ms. Pac-Man, so it's my turn.

"They're scary."

"Yeah, but they were blocking the entrance." She cocks her head to the side. "What happened? You told off Joe."

"Yeah, but . . ."

"But what?" Liat asks.

"Joe's a little shrimp," I reply.

"And . . ."

And I can't think of anything else to say.

chapter twelve

when we get back from the mall, I see a red, white, and blue U.S. Mail truck at the end of our block. I race to our mailbox and feel my heart explode when I see a pale-blue aeromail envelope peeking out from under all the other mail.

"A letter from *Ema*!" Gayle screeches from behind me, grabbing the letter out of the mailbox before I can. She closes her fist around it and starts dancing on the lawn.

"Give me that!" I shriek, trying to snatch it out of her hands.

Gayle giggles and takes off. I run after her. We run around our whole house three times before we're both completely beat. When I catch up to Gayle, I'm almost too tired to even take the letter from her, but I do anyway. She doesn't put up a fight, and the envelope slides easily out of her grasp.

I rip it open, but I know even before I look inside that it will be a complete waste of time. As I expect, there are no vowels. It looks like a chicken dipped its feet into black ink and skated haphazardly across the blue sheet of paper.

I realize Liat has been watching us quietly all this time. I guess I kind of forgot about her in the excitement of finding *Ema*'s letter.

Liat looks upset. In fact, she looks like she's about to cry.

"Are you okay?" I ask her.

She nods once, but in a way that says she doesn't want talk about it. She turns her face away from me and takes several deep swallows of air.

It hits me.

Her mom. Our mom being alive—and hers being dead. I feel terrible about this, but I don't know what to do.

Aba watches us quietly too. Because I don't know what else to do, I walk up to him, give him the letter, and ask him to read it. So, he does, right there, right then, while all of us are standing on the lawn.

It says all the usual things: *Ema* misses us, she'll come home soon, she thinks about us every minute of every day. And yet, it sounds rushed, and I wonder if it is rushed.

I wonder if maybe that's why *Ema* doesn't take the time to put in vowels anymore. I wonder if she's dashing off these letters as fast as possible.

Why?

To get them over with? To get this troublesome chore over with as soon as possible?

It makes my stomach sink into my knees.

Is *Ema* . . . forgetting us? Is her sister more important to her than we are?

Aba says he has to get ready for work. I know he's already delayed past the time he'd normally go, but I wish, just for once, he'd stay home with us. Do some normal American thing with us like make popcorn and hot cocoa and play checkers.

My wish isn't granted.

Aba leaves for work.

Liat, Gayle, and I sit aimlessly on our stoop. *Ema*'s letter is clutched in Gayle's hands. She passes it to Liat.

"Can you read this to us?" she asks. "I need to hear it again."

I guess Gayle assumes, like I do, that Liat is good at reading Hebrew.

But Liat says, "I don't read well without vowels. My dad could read it for you, but he's working, too, like your dad." She seems really bummed out. Her voice is soft and her eyes are shiny—like she's holding back tears.

I'm bummed out, too. I don't even feel like watching TV.

The day stretches out before us in all its depressing splendor.

I don't know how we're going to get through it.

chapter thirteen

liat says, "hey, i know. Let's do a night of wings.
That'll cheer us up." Her voice is still soft, but I can
tell she's trying to sound happy.

This is a perfect idea, and I'm all for it. Besides,
Liat did promise she'd teach me how to make wings.

We set up shop in my room. Liat brings hot rollers,
a curling iron, and beauty magazines from her house. I
think they all belong to Rivka. Gayle lies on the floor,
flipping through the magazines. I sit on a chair in front

of my mirror and Liat stands behind me, like in a beauty salon.

I know what hot rollers and curling irons are, but I've never actually used them. Whenever I attempted to make wings, I used our blow dryer and my round brush. No wonder it didn't work out.

"You've got to have the right tools," Liat says when I tell her about my failed attempts. "That's the secret."

"My father always says that," I say.

"About curling irons and hot rollers?"

"No," I reply with a smile. "About doing stuff around the house. You know, hammers and saws and things like that."

"Well, he's right," Liat says.

"Yeah," I murmur. "I guess he is."

Almost Mike-Brady-and-Pa-Ingalls-right.

Liat begins rolling my hair. She gives instructions as she goes. Soon we've stopped feeling so bummed out.

"You're lucky you have Rivka," I say. "To show you how to do your hair and stuff."

Liat clips a curler into place. "I'd rather have my mother," she says quietly.

I don't know what to say. "I'm sorry about your mother," I mumble. Then I add, "My mother's been gone for three months."

"At least you have a mother," Liat says.

"Yeah, but she's in Israel."

"At least she's not dead," Liat responds.

This statement gives me chills. And it makes me suddenly worry about bombings in Israel. I'm eager to change the subject, so I ask, "Do people, like, live in igloos in Alaska?"

She laughs. "No, we lived in, like, a regular city. Anchorage." She adds slyly, "It even has a mall."

"So, are people the same in all the places you've lived?"

Liat carefully tucks another curler in place. "What do you mean?"

"I mean, are there people who are . . . mean and nasty in Alaska?"

"Sure," Liat says with a shrug. "There are mean and nasty people everywhere."

"Even in Alaska?"

"Yup, even in Alaska."

"So, every place is the same?"

Liat ponders this. "Well, yes and no. Alaska's different from Florida. And Ohio's different from Texas. But people are mostly the same."

I ask, "How come you're not scared to start a new school?"

Liat shrugs. "I guess I've done it a zillion times."

"But what about starting all over, making new friends, not getting picked on . . ."

Liat shrugs. "Yeah, it's hard."

"Were you ever picked on?"

"Yeah, definitely," she says.

"Really?" I ask, turning in my seat. I find this impossible.

Liat places her hands on my head to steady my curls. "Yeah, lots of times."

"What did you do?"

"Tried to make them stop."

"How?"

"All different ways," she says mysteriously.

"Like what?" I ask desperately. Of all the questions I've asked, this one is the most important.

Liat stops what she's doing. "It's more of an

attitude," she says. "It's hard to explain. It's like—the way you think about yourself."

I try to understand this as she begins unclipping the curlers. "We're almost there," she says, brushing out my hair and taking care of any loose spots with the curling iron.

"Ta-da!" she announces at last. "I give you: Wings."

I actually gasp. I have wings! Two perfect, glorious wings!

"Wow," I whisper, fingering them delicately. "They're beautiful."

"Yeah, but look how long it took to make them, Roxanne," Liat replies, checking her watch.

"It's totally worth it," I declare.

Liat looks into my eyes in the mirror's reflection. "I don't know. . . . Some things are more important than wings."

"Nothing's more important than wings," I shoot back.

Liat eyes me intensely. "Really?"

I shut up then.

chapter fourteen

halloween is a big deal on our block.

All the little kids wear costumes and go trick-or-treating. We do, too. Eighth grade is the unofficial cut-off point. Afterward, when it gets dark, everyone hikes to the woods to tell ghost stories.

Kathleen, Gayle, Liat, and I plan to go trick-or-treating together. We go to Liat's house to pick her up.

Kathleen is dressed as a witch, in a sheer black dress and torn black stockings. Her pointed black hat keeps flopping over her forehead. It annoys her a lot, but at least she has a different costume from last year.

Gayle and I dress as black cats, same as last year. Black headbands with furry black ears, fuzzy black tails, and black noses with black whiskers.

Secretly, I wish I could go as Wonder Woman.

It's hard to think of Liat's house as Liat's house and not the Cursed House. Especially since it's Halloween. I find myself wondering if there are secret torture chambers behind the walls, dusty dungeons in the basement, crumbling skeletons under the floor, and bloody body parts in the attic. It makes me shudder—scared and excited at the same time.

Rivka answers the door. She's wearing a long wine-colored dress with jagged sleeves. I wonder if this is a special outfit for Halloween or if it's for everyday use. I decide it's the latter.

Rivka screeches in delight. "*Eizeh yoffee!*" she cries, which means "How lovely!"

Liat's father comes to the door. He's wearing yet another polyester special. He must have a limitless supply. It looks appropriate today, though. It is, after all, Halloween.

Liat doesn't have a costume. Rivka helps her throw

together some clothes and says she's going as a "weirdo." I want to laugh at that one. Will the real weirdo please stand up?

In the end, Liat wears a sparkly blue wig, shiny black pants, a gold shirt with silver stripes, and red cowboy boots. Everything is borrowed from Rivka. Ha! No surprise there. Rivka makes up Liat's eyes so heavily with silver eye shadow and black eyeliner that she looks like Cleopatra. She looks really pretty.

Every Halloween, the same rumor goes around the block that somebody is giving away green apples with razor blades wedged inside them. I have never once gotten a green apple from anyone on Halloween, but the rumor still goes around every year. The boys love telling the little kids on the block what will happen to their mouths and tongues and throats when they bite into it.

Rivka invites us inside and fills our bags with plastic-wrapped *baklava* that she informs us has just come out of the oven. I don't think Rivka understands that Halloween is all about store-bought, sealed candy. Well, at least it isn't green apples. You could expect something like that from the Cursed House.

In the living room, I notice a photo on the wall of a black-haired woman sitting on a flowered towel at the beach. Next to her is a little girl with the same black hair. I study the picture closely until it finally dawns on me. It's Liat and her mom.

"That was our last vacation—the last time we were all together," Liat says, coming up behind me. "We went to Elat."

I nod solemnly. It's hard to take Liat seriously with her sparkly blue hair and Cleopatra eyes, but there's no mistaking the deep sorrow in her voice. I want to hug her, but I worry Liat won't like it. It occurs to me that my parents went to Elat on their honeymoon. I don't really know anything about Elat. I only know what my parents have told me—that it's like Israel's Miami Beach.

I pry my eyes away from the photo and look around the living room. The furniture Liat and her father have is shabby, which possibly means they're poorer than us.

The longer I stand there, the more freaked-out I start to feel. If anything bad is going to happen in this house, it will surely be on Halloween. I'm relieved when Rivka tells us, "Have good time—don't eat so much bad stuff," and sends us off.

We go trick-or-treating for two and a half hours, stuffing ourselves as we go along with Snickers and Milky Ways and Tootsie Rolls and M&M's and Butterfingers. I start to feel sick. I never want to look at another candy bar again. Then, holding our stomachs, we head to the woods as night falls.

No one has given us green apples, though someone did give chocolate chip cookies in sandwich baggies. It's too bad, because I love chocolate chip cookies.

"How could they be so clueless?" Gayle complains, tossing her cookies into a trash can. "What a waste."

"I wouldn't get rid of them if I were you," I say, feeling mischievous. "You might need them to feed the werewolves."

"Werewolves?" she asks fearfully.

"Haven't you heard? There were reports last week of three werewolves in the woods," I say, then mimic a round of evil laughter like the villains on *Super Friends*.

Gayle rolls her eyes.

I sound much, much more lighthearted than I actually feel. I do not like the woods, even during the day. I'm ready to head home, but Kathleen wants to go there. Last year, I was sure I was going to have a heart attack during the telling of the ghost stories. Nothing happened, but I was glad when it was over. Why does Halloween have to be about ghosts and witches and vampires? Why can't it just be about free candy?

We reach the woods. Kathleen brought a flashlight from home, and we walk slowly behind the faint beam. In the dark, the trees strongly resemble murderers and kidnappers. Disturbing thoughts from every horror movie I've ever seen race through my mind as we crunch the dried leaves. I see brain-dead zombies in every shadow. A sudden breeze feels icy on my bare neck. Every time a branch snags me, I am convinced it is an escaped convict with a long, sharp knife.

We look for the clearing, where everyone is supposed to meet. Some kids believe the strange clearing in the middle of the woods is where the aliens landed in their spaceship when they arrived to kidnap people for their wicked medical experiments. I have to admit it is odd to have a perfect clearing right in the middle of the woods, but I'm sure it has nothing to do with evil aliens. Right?

Someone lets out a bloodcurdling wail.

Before I know what's happening, I'm grabbed roughly around the waist. I shriek my head off as the person—or thing!—drags me away from the others and pulls me down to the ground. A warm mouth suddenly closes over mine.

Is this a kiss?

The warm lips pull back.

"Kathleen?" the mouth says.

"Eddie?" I croak.

He stands up. Blue eyes twinkle at me. He is dressed as a skeleton in a tight-fitting black bodysuit with white bones gleaming against it. My entire body burns with embarrassment and shame.

"Roxanne?" he mutters. Then, sheepishly, "Sorry, I thought you were Kathleen."

Kathleen, Gayle, and Liat soon surround me. I get to my feet slowly, feeling dazed.

"Are you okay?" Liat asks.

"Um, yeah," I mumble. "I'm okay." I can't make myself look at Eddie.

"What did you grab Roxanne for?" Kathleen asks, punching him in the arm.

Kathleen didn't see the kiss! I ask myself if it really happened or if I just imagined it.

Eddie ignores Kathleen's question. "Come on, let's go," he says briskly. He seizes Kathleen's hand and begins leading her through the woods. Kathleen doesn't pull her hand away from his. I feel a sharp pang of jealousy.

I shuffle behind everyone, licking my lips slowly. I wonder how a boy's lips could feel so soft, so sweet. My first kiss! From Eddie!

Except that it was meant for Kathleen. I try to forget that part.

We reach the clearing. Kids are milling around. Some are seated in a circle on the ground. We find a free spot and sit down together. I sit between Eddie and Liat, feeling a strange mixture of euphoria and envy.

Eddie grabs Kathleen's flashlight and holds it under his chin. The light makes him look like a hideous zombie. His blue eyes glitter when he glances at me. I feel that same burning sensation of lust and humiliation.

"Let's begin," he says in a deep, exaggerated voice. "Gather round, my maggots, and we will talk about horror and blood and guts."

Everyone sits down and gazes at him expectantly. Lots of kids have brought flashlights, and they hold them under their chins like Eddie. The circle looks like a spooky ring of bobbing zombie heads.

"As you all know, horrible creatures live in these woods," Eddie says ominously. "Creatures who feast on brains and suck blood out of veins and peck eyeballs out of skulls."

Kids make delighted grossed-out sounds.

"Last year I found the skeleton of Stood-Up Serena in these woods," Eddie goes on somberly. "Stood-Up Serena was tortured before she was murdered in these woods. They pulled out her fingernails, cut off her nose, sliced off her ears, popped out her eyeballs, and chopped off her toes one by one."

The taste of six different candy bars rises up in my throat, but I swallow furiously. I know Eddie is making all this up, but does he have to be so disgusting?

Eddie suddenly stops and looks meaningfully at Liat. "We have among us tonight a descendant of Stood-Up Serena."

An excited murmur travels around the circle.

"This descendant has moved into the Cursed House, that place of horror and evil, to accept the same fate of her long-lost ancestor."

Kathleen sighs loudly and tries snatching the flashlight away from Eddie. But Eddie resists and continues to talk about the Cursed House, recounting in graphic detail all the bloody things that have happened there. He also adds some imaginative stories of his own involving chain saws, axes, ice picks, and black crows with sharp beaks.

Goose bumps on my arms and legs sprout into Mount Everests. Some kids in the creepy, zombie-head circle squirm uneasily. Others sniffle in low voices.

I glance at Liat. Her face is expressionless.

We hear loud thrashing noises. Eddie stops talk-ing. A bunch of Things suddenly crash out of the woods and into the clearing. The zombie-head circle erupts in screams. Kids jump up and run in all direc-tions. The Things reach out arms and grab at people. Eddie shines his flashlight onto them.

It's red-bumped-pimply-faced Glenn! And his red-bumped-pimply-faced friends!

I scramble to my feet and, without even devoting one ounce of brain activity to the thought, take off. I ignore twisted branches scratching at my arms and face. I trip over a log, fall facedown into a pile of crud, get up, and take off again. Not until I'm at the edge of the woods do I stop running. I'm surprised to see Gayle and Liat beside me. We're all panting.

"I can't believe . . . we just left like that," Liat says.

Not very Wonder Woman–like. I feel totally uncool.

chapter fifteen

it's the day after halloween. Gayle and I are having candy bars for breakfast, but they're bitter, not sweet, on my tongue.

I'm thinking about Liat.

Liat and I are the same age, we came to the U.S. at exactly the same time, and we both have strange Israeli parents (except for her not having a mother).

And yet.

I am afraid.

Embarrassed.

Confused.

Liat is not.

The sound of the doorbell interrupts my thoughts. I open the door to find Liat and Rivka standing on our stoop. Rivka is wearing a neon-orange top, dark pink pants, and deep-purple cowboy boots. She is so bright I have to squint. Liat is carrying a foil-wrapped plate.

"Rivka made this," Liat says, handing me the plate. "It's her fantastic *schnitzel*."

"Just for you, *booba*!" Rivka screeches.

It smells wonderful. "Thank you," I say. *Schnitzel* isn't a real Hebrew word, but for some reason, it's the word most Israelis use for fried chicken.

"I go now," Rivka says. "I have perm twins today." Her boots click smartly on the sidewalk as she hurries away.

I take the plate from Liat. It's very American, when you think about it, to bring food to your neighbors. Funny that Rivka, who is so Israeli, would do that.

"What are perm twins?" I ask as I carry the plate carefully into the kitchen and set it on the table. Gayle's still gorging herself on a Snickers bar.

Liat follows me. "Oh, these cute little twin girls are getting perms today," she says.

Gayle sniffs loudly. "What's that?" she asks.

The scent of fried chicken has filled every crevice of the kitchen. Although I'm not hungry, I peel back the foil from the plate and gaze appreciatively at the golden-brown pieces. Gayle removes a leg and chomps down on it. Liat and I sit at the table and watch her.

"Rivka's a great cook," Gayle says between bites.

"Yeah, Rivka's great," Liat agrees.

"Too bad she isn't so great with clothes," I say.

"What's wrong with her clothes?" Liat asks.

I grunt. "Haven't you noticed?"

Liat shrugs. "They're not so bad. A little bright, I guess."

I ask the question I've been wanting to ask for a long time. "How come your dad wears those outfits?"

Gayle wipes chicken juice from her mouth and looks expectantly at Liat.

Liat shrugs again. "I guess they're comfortable."

"But they make him look so weird. Like Rivka."

"So?"

"So, aren't you worried?"

"About what?"

"About people staring at them? About being embarrassed when you're with them?"

"Maybe a little bit," she admits.

"What if someone called Rivka a weirdo while you were with her?" I ask, getting to the point.

"I guess I'd ignore them."

"What if they started a fight with you?" I ask.

"I'd fight back, Roxanne."

"What if you didn't know how to fight back?"

"I'd learn." Liat leans forward. "We're Israeli, Roxanne. Israelis are tough. Israelis are *sabras*."

Sabra is Hebrew for "prickly pear," a tropical fruit that grows in Israel. Sabras are tough and hard on the outside, soft and sweet on the inside.

I want to be a *sabra*.

The TV suddenly goes blank. An announcer says they are interrupting their regularly scheduled program to bring us a news alert. A man with silver hair starts talking about Israel. We all freeze and glue our eyes to the screen.

"We've just gotten word that a bomb has killed a dozen people in Jerusalem earlier this morning. No one has claimed responsibility. . . ."

The words melt together in my ears. The only thing I'm able to concentrate on is the horrible pictures on TV. People spattered with bright red blood, people weeping, people running, people screaming, people lying on the ground, reaching their arms toward the camera. . . .

"*Ema*," Gayle murmurs.

What did the announcer say? Jerusalem?

Ema isn't in Jerusalem. *Ema* is in Tel Aviv.

"She's in Tel Aviv," I say, my voice sounding far away. "She's not in Jerusalem."

But I wonder. What if she went to Jerusalem? What if she decided to visit Jerusalem? What if she was in Jerusalem? What if, what if, what if she's one of those people, those people spattered with bright red blood, those people weeping, those people running, those people screaming, those people lying on the ground, reaching their arms toward the camera. . . .

I'm distracted from these terrible thoughts by loud wails. Loud wails in the kitchen. Gayle is crying, her cheeks are splotchy and scarlet, tears are rolling down her cheeks, her expression is twisted into utter agony.

I put my arms around her. Her entire body shakes uncontrollably. Tears burn in my eyes, too, but a voice inside my head keeps saying, "She's not in Jerusalem. She's in Tel Aviv. In Tel Aviv. Not Jerusalem. Tel Aviv. Not Jerusalem."

I'm surprised when I look up. Liat is shaking, too. Shaking just like Gayle. Her face is splotchy, too, twisted like my sister's, shiny with tears. Is Liat . . .

Crying?

Strong, tough, Israeli Liat?

It's a silent kind of crying, but it's crying.

Liat is crying for my *ema*?

No.

Liat is crying for her *ema*.

The voice inside my head, the one that insisted *Ema* isn't one of those people, is overcome by the wailing in the kitchen, and soon I'm crying, too. The three of us are bawling, right there in the kitchen, with the TV blaring, the announcer talking, sirens yowling, pictures flashing, and those people in Jerusalem screaming and weeping and dying, and I can't take it, I can't take it.

Aba said we could call *Ema* in an emergency. This is an emergency.

With Gayle still in my arms, I half-drag and half-carry her to the telephone on the wall. I try to remember how to dial Israel, but I'm too upset. It takes three tries before I get all the numbers right.

There is a lot of static and clicking and noise. But I hear a single voice ask, "Hello?"

I feel life drain back into my body.

"*Ema!*" I holler. "You're alive!"

"*Motek!* Yes, *motek*, oh, I miss you so much. I try to call before but the lines were blocked. I knew you would worry. I'm in Tel Aviv. I am okay."

"I miss you!" I yell, and, all of a sudden, I'm crying even harder.

Gayle grabs the telephone from me and screams, "*Ema*, I want you to come home!"

"Soon," *Ema* says. "I am okay. I love you so much."

The static comes again, and the call is over.

An obnoxious dial tone drones in my ears.

Gayle smiles up at me through her wet eyelashes. I kiss her cheek.

Liat is wiping her eyes delicately, carefully, as if she's wearing Cleopatra makeup.

"Liat . . . ," I start to say, but I can't think of any words that will help.

chapter sixteen

things feel very strange between me and Liat
for a few days after the Jerusalem bombing. In fact, we
even get into another little fight.

It happens when Gayle and I are watching cartoons in our pajamas on Saturday morning. Liat rings
the doorbell. We let her in and she sighs, "You guys
watch so much TV."

"So?" I ask.

"So," Liat answers, "why don't you do something
instead?"

"Watching TV is doing something," I reply.

Liat shakes her head. "Watching TV is doing nothing."

"It's not nothing!" I say, my voice rising. "TV is great! TV is better than real life! On TV things are the way they're supposed to be! On TV the bad guys always get beaten up!"

I don't mean to say these things—or to say them in such a loud, angry way—but they describe exactly how I feel.

Silence falls. Liat says nothing. Gayle says nothing. I say nothing.

Finally, after what feels like hours, Liat says, "Rivka has the day off today. She wants to know if you want makeovers."

"Makeovers?" I ask, perking up.

"Yeah, she can do them at my house."

Why didn't Liat just say so? Why'd she have to go and get into a fight with me over watching TV? Of course I want a makeover!

I wonder how I'm going to resolve this, but then Liat asks, "So, you guys want to do that?" and I say, "Yeah," and Gayle says, "Yeah," and that's it. We're all okay. A little while later, Gayle and I are both dressed and at Liat's house. It's so weird how Liat just lets things go—not that I'm complaining.

"We going to give you complete makeover," Rivka pronounces when I sit down in a chair in the kitchen. There is a mirror on a silver stand on the kitchen table in front of me, the kind they have at makeup counters at the mall, and lots of tubes and bottles and brushes and sponges. Liat and Gayle sit at the table, too, awaiting their turns and watching me closely—as if *I'm* a TV show.

Rivka buzzes around me, the sleeves of her shirt trailing behind her like two green snakes. She is decked out completely in bright-green leather—pants, boots, and vest. Her green shirt is made of a soft, sheer material. The sleeves are flowing and puffy.

I'm excited about having a makeover, but I'm not sure about Rivka. What if I end up looking like a circus clown? Rivka is not exactly subtle.

"Can I go after Roxanne?" Gayle asks as she absently picks up a tube of beige liquid and turns it over curiously in her hands.

"Yes, yes, we all going to have a turn, just be patience," Rivka says.

I wonder if I should correct her English, but I decide not to. I don't want to distract her.

Liat's got a small smile on her face. I wonder what she's thinking.

Rivka begins to apply a tan-colored lotion to my face. "You know, when I your age, I don't know how put on makeup either."

Even though Rivka's broken English is severe, I have no trouble understanding her. "Did you grow up in Israel?" I ask.

"Sure, yes," she answers with a smile. "In Haifa. I have eleven brothers and sisters. My mother never have time to show me makeup. She too busy."

"How did you learn?" I ask.

Rivka takes a small sponge and taps my face with it. "I learn from magazines, from friends. Then I go to school to be beautician." She puts down the sponge and picks up a long black pencil.

I want to ask her about this, but Rivka begins writing on my eyes with the pencil. I know she's not really writing, but that's what it feels like. It's too uncomfortable to talk with her poking my eyes like that.

"I remember when I your age, I get my *tzitzim* and my mother, she not even talk to me about it."

Gayle starts to giggle. *Tzitzim* means "breasts."

"I hate my *tzitzim* so much," Rivka says. "I no want them. I tell my mother to sell them."

"Sell them?" Gayle bursts out.

"Yes," Rivka responds, at last putting down the pencil. "I no want them. I so, how you say, embarrassed. But, you know, I grow up and now I love my *tzitzim*."

Gayle and Liat crack up with laughter. Rivka chooses a rosy brown eye shadow and begins applying it to my eyelids. "Israelis no talk about things like this. Not like Americans."

She puts down the eye shadow and picks up a pink bottle of mascara. As she brushes my eyelashes with the mascara, and I try not to blink too much, she goes on. "Americans, they talk about everything. They come and sit in chair and tell me about problems, marriages, kids, jobs. They tell me they have this disease and that disease."

She puts down the mascara bottle and picks up a fluffy brush. She dips it into a red-orange powder and dabs my cheeks with it. "Israelis, they keep everything inside. They no talk like Americans." She puts the brush away and picks up a tube of red lipstick. "Israelis, they tough. But inside, they soft like mush." She outlines my lips with the lipstick, then fills them in. I notice Gayle studying my face in fascination.

"Okay," Rivka says. "We done." She adjusts the mirror so I can look into it.

I gasp. The girl staring back at me is . . . beautiful.

She has rosy cheeks, full red lips, and striking dark eyes.

"Roxanne, you look like a model," Gayle whispers.

"She beautiful, no?" Rivka asks.

"Extremely," Liat answers.

I can't help smiling.

chapter seventeen

i wish i could wear makeup and wings every
day, but Liat is right. It would take an extra two hours
every morning, and, as much as I want it, I can't make
myself get up that early, especially after being up late
waiting for *Aba*. I wonder if Donna and her friends rise
at dawn to make themselves look that good.

Meanwhile, in gym, the torture continues.

Outdoor softball. Donna is captain again.

"Liat," she says.

Liat is picked first.

Liat doesn't move. Instead of joining Donna, she studies her fingernails.

"Liat," Donna says again, a bit more loudly.

"Only if you pick Roxanne next," Liat says without looking up.

I jerk my head toward her. Huh?

Donna narrows her eyes. "What did you say?" she asks.

Liat looks up calmly. "I said, only if you pick Roxanne next."

Donna looks from Liat to me. Her cheeks redden.

"Rachel," she says firmly.

Rachel hesitates.

"Rachel," Donna says again. Rachel glances at Liat, then steps out of the line to join Donna. Everyone is picked off until it's me, Liat, Gheeta, and Suri—the Official Society of Gym Losers.

I allow myself to sneak a look at Liat and wonder what on Earth she's doing. Instead of feeling flattered, I'm horrified. I hate the attention she's drawn to me.

"Gheeta," I hear.

"Suri," I hear next.

"Roxanne," Donna says, throwing me a dirty look.

That leaves Liat standing there alone. They don't even call her. She walks to the other team while I shuffle miserably to Donna's team.

I didn't think it was possible, but gym has sunk to a new low.

I mill around the outfield aimlessly, not knowing what to think:

a. martians landed on liat's roof last night and performed a lobotomy as she slept?
b. the curse has struck liat for certain doom by donna?
c. liat's doing this on purpose because she has some kind of insane plan in mind?

Liat's an unstoppable softball machine. I've never seen anyone play better. She annihilates Donna's team.

"Great game," girls gush, crowding around Liat as we jog to the locker room afterward.

"Yeah, great game," Donna says with both sarcasm and admiration. The other girls automatically scatter as Donna edges toward us, like Moses parting the Red Sea.

Donna's holding a carefully folded denim jacket over one arm. It's her boyfriend's jacket. There's a painting of Ozzy Osbourne on the back.

Liat walks casually to her locker.

"Hey," Donna says.

Liat doesn't answer.

"Hey," Donna says again, then adds, "Yo, Liat."

"What?" Liat asks in annoyance.

I think I may pass out.

"I'm sneaking out for a cig," Donna says. "Will you watch my jacket for me?"

Liat studies the jacket. "Can I wear it?" she asks.

Donna seems taken aback. "Okay," she says. "If you take care of it." She holds out the jacket.

"Can Roxanne wear it, too?" Liat asks.

I have to stop myself from screaming.

Donna's obviously trying to make up with Liat, because Liat's a great athlete and Donna needs her on her team from now on. So she's offering Liat her greatest possession.

Donna gazes at me hatefully, then pulls the jacket back toward her. "No," she says. "Never mind."

Liat shrugs nonchalantly.

This seems to make Donna even madder. She takes a step forward. Her face is contorted with rage and shame. "I'll see you after school," she growls, giving Liat a meaningful look. She walks away.

An icy shudder travels up and down my spine.

Oh. No.

"Are you crazy?" I hiss at Liat, raising my arms in a hopeless gesture. "Do you know what you just did?"

"You said TV was better than real life," Liat replies fiercely. "You said the bad guys always get beaten up."

"Yeah," I answer, "so?"

"So, that happens in real life, too."

"Liat," I say desperately, "you've gone mental."

Liat lets out a chuckle.

"It's not funny!" I snap. "Donna was trying to be nice to you! Now there's going to be a fight after school!"

"Donna's just using me," Liat says.

"Now there's going to be a fight after school!" I repeat. I bend down, placing my head between my legs, and close my eyes. "I think I'm going to be sick."

Liat touches my arm. "You don't need to do any-thing, Roxanne. You just watch it like it's on TV."

I don't know whether to feel insulted or relieved by this statement. I go through the rest of the school day numb. I'm faintly aware of Liat walking next to me. I avoid Donna as much as possible. I pretend it's all just a bad dream. I almost believe it, too.

Until the last school bell rings.

It's like a signal has been given. How does word of a fight travel so fast? A mob of kids has gathered in an empty lot four blocks from school. It's like a carnival or something. I feel like someone should sell cotton candy and corn dogs.

ladies and gentlemen!
a must-see girl fight!
we give you: liat versus donna!

I trudge behind a group of talkative girls, my stom-ach doing flip-flops. Some of the kids in the mob are chanting, "Fight! Fight! Fight!" I stand on the edge of the crowd, looking in the direction of the school, wondering what would happen if I barged into the main office and told them there was a fight four blocks away. Would the principal gallop over to break it up? Or would Silver-Haired Mutant just shrug at me?

All after-school fights take place in this empty lot. Usually it's boys fighting over girls. But girls fight dirtier. Everybody knows that. Boys have an honor code. Girls don't. They'll gouge each other's eyeballs out with keys, rings, or anything else they can get their polished pink fingernails on.

I push my way through the thick crowd until I'm standing in front. Liat and Donna are hanging out on opposite sides of a circle like two boxers waiting for the first bell. I wonder if Liat knows I'm here. As if to answer my question, Liat turns her head in my direction. When she spots me, she nods. My stomach starts to hurt.

I wish someone would step out of the circle and say, "Let's not resort to violence. Let's talk this thing out."

But nobody does. Instead, the chanting just gets louder. It's driving me crazy. Just when I think I can't take another second, Liat and Donna draw closer to one another. The chants die down. I force myself to keep my eyes open.

Liat and Donna circle each other like those animals on nature shows. Then suddenly they come together like two wrestlers. They twist and rock and push and pull. Liat kicks out her leg sharply. It lands behind Donna's knees. Donna falls instantly to the ground.

The crowd gasps. Liat stands over Donna, waiting for her to get up. But Donna doesn't. She landed hard on the concrete. It occurs to me that she might have hit her head.

Seconds tick by. Donna is clearly hurt. Two of her friends approach her sprawled body and lift her off the ground. Donna looks like she's dead. But she blinks open her eyes, rubs her head, and winces in pain. The girls drag Donna away like a limp doll between them.

Just like that, the fight's over. It barely lasted a minute.

I stare hard at Liat, and, all of a sudden, I see Wonder Woman standing there, her scarlet cape flaring out behind her, her black hair blowing in the wind.

chapter eighteen

my hands don't sweat in gym anymore.

It's quite mysterious.

I know it has something to do with Liat. I know it has *everything* to do with Liat.

See, I'm not afraid as much.

Of Donna. Of the ball. Of not being athletic.

Don't get me wrong. I still very much support a congressional ban on gym. And I still wish someone would blow it up. But it doesn't *torture* me like it used to.

I ask Liat where she learned that kicking move that brought Donna down so quickly.

"From my dad," she says. "If you kick someone behind their knees, they'll lose their footing instantly. It's the fastest way to make someone fall."

"Where did your dad learn it?" I ask.

"The army," Liat says.

My dad served in the Israeli army, too. Everyone in Israel has to serve when they turn eighteen—men and women. *Tzava*, they call it, which means "army," or *Tzahal*, which is the Hebrew abbreviation for I.D.F.—Israel Defense Forces. You can't go anywhere in Israel without seeing all the soldiers in their olive uniforms, long guns slung over their shoulders.

I've never asked my dad about his army experience. I don't even know what he did—what unit he was in, where he served, whether he fought in any wars.

The next time we're at the mall in the noisy food court, I ask. "*Aba*, what did you do in the army?"

"I was radio officer," he answers.

"What's that?"

"I send messages."

"You mean like Morse code?"

"Yes," he says.

"You know Morse code?"

"Yes."

"Isn't it hard?" I ask.

"No, not really."

"Did you fight in any wars?" I ask.

"I was in Sinai in 1967."

"The Six-Day War?"

"Yes."

I'm silent. My dad fought in an actual war, and I never even knew about it. I ask him softly, "Did you and *Ema* go to Elat on your honeymoon?"

Aba's eyes brighten. "Oh, yes. Beautiful place. Like heaven."

"You think . . . we'll ever go there?"

"Yes," *Aba* says excitedly. "If you want to. I think you should visit Israel."

I cough. "How come we don't talk about Israel hardly ever?"

Aba frowns. "Because we want you to be American."

I lower my head. All this time I thought my parents

got in my way of being American, but it's actually something they want, too. It's something I should've known, just like my dad fighting in a war.

Nobody wants to be American more than me. But I can't pretend I wasn't born in Israel. I'm a *sabra*.

"Maybe we can talk about it a little," I say. "Maybe you could . . . help me read Hebrew without vowels."

"Sure," *Aba* replies with a smile.

I pause, then whisper, "Liat's mother died in a bombing."

"Yes," *Aba* says, lowering his eyes.

"I hope *Ema* doesn't die," I say.

"No," he says sharply. "She will come home soon."

chapter nineteen

it's been more than a month since Liat moved
into the Cursed House, and a strange thing has happened.
Kids on the block have stopped wondering when something terrible is going to happen to her and her father.

Gayle and I discuss this phenomenon while we
play Legos in the basement on a Sunday afternoon.
Legos in the basement is a game we've played since
forever. But don't get the wrong idea. We're not like
those child geniuses who build sprawling Lego metro-
polises with highways and harbors and airports.

Gayle and I use mismatched pieces of Legos to make two best friends, Dale and Lulu. Dale is blond (we use a yellow Lego piece for her hair) and Lulu is brunette (a blue Lego piece, since we don't have a brown one). Dale and Lulu wear designer clothes; have rich parents, perfect wings, fancy red convertibles, and plenty of food in their kitchens; and go to lots of places with their cute boyfriends.

We use special high-pitched voices to speak as Dale and Lulu. We don't find these voices especially funny, but they'd probably sound utterly insane to anyone unfamiliar with our game.

"Let's go to the city to see *Cats* on Broadway," Gayle squeals in her Lulu voice.

"Yes," I squeak as Dale, "let's change into our party gowns." This means using clear Lego pieces for the girls' skirts instead of the red pieces they normally wear. Clear is supposed to stand for silver or diamond.

Lulu says, "We'll go to dinner first. At a fancy restaurant in Chinatown."

"Yes," Dale squawks. "It'll be fun! But who should I invite?"

"Well," Lulu says, "let's think. Who's been really good this week?"

"Hmmm," Dale muses. "Bo sent me a dozen roses yesterday. And Luke bought me a diamond necklace. But Lancelot asked me to marry him. He's going to build us a beautiful pink house."

Gayle stares at me. I sit back on my heels. I can't believe I just said that.

"A *pink* house?" Gayle asks in a low voice. Then she looks right at me and asks, "Roxanne, do you think . . . the Curse is over?"

I take a deep breath. "I don't know," I reply truthfully.

It's something I've pondered. But I've come to the conclusion that just because nothing has happened in the past month doesn't mean nothing will *ever* happen. I'm sure there were families who lived in the house longer than a month before the Curse struck. Didn't Stood-Up Serena live in the house for years before she vanished in the woods on the night of the senior prom?

Gayle turns her attention back to Lulu. "Maybe you want a beautiful *blue* house instead," she squeals.

"Yes," I squeak back. "A beautiful blue house with three swimming pools, two tennis courts, and seven rose gardens. Oh, darling Lancelot, I will marry you." I make smoochy noises.

At that moment, I hear footsteps.

I instinctively gaze up at the grimy basement window and see four sneaker-clad feet scurry away.

Gayle's mouth drops open.

"Did they hear us?" I ask in a whisper.

Gayle looks stricken. She drops Lulu and bolts for the stairs. A moment later, she has run up to her room and slammed the door.

My face feels hot. Whoever was spying on us surely heard me accepting a marriage proposal in a high-pitched voice from a piece of Lego.

Footsteps sound on the basement stairs. Kathleen and Liat come bouncing down. They seem amused.

I gaze at them through narrowed eyes. "You were spying on us," I say.

The expression on Kathleen's face gets more amused. "We weren't spying," she says playfully.

Liat seems less smug. "We just asked your dad where you were. He said in the basement. He said to go through the back."

It figures that the one Sunday my father is home changing the oil in his taxi, Liat and Kathleen would show up.

Kathleen's eyes twinkle. "Oh, darling Lancelot!" she suddenly bursts out.

"Shut up, Kathleen," I say.

"My beautiful Lancelot!" she goes on.

"Shut up," I say again, then add, "Get out."

Liat lifts her hand as if she's directing traffic. "Look, it's okay. We just wanted to know if you want to come to town. We could get spice cakes."

I shake my head back and forth. "Get out," I repeat.

Kathleen, grinning, starts to make her way back up the stairs.

"Nice friend," I say, watching her leave.

Liat frowns at me. "She's still your friend, Roxanne. She's just teasing you."

"Yeah, right," I sputter.

Liat sighs. She seems exasperated. "Roxanne, you're too worried about people making fun of you. Or beating you up."

I stare at her in disbelief. " 'Cause it hurts!" I yell. "Getting made fun of hurts! Getting beaten up hurts!"

Liat's face reddens. "No," she says angrily. "Having your mom blown to pieces hurts." She looks away. "That hurts so bad, everything else is nothing."

A silence settles between us. Liat's statement has knocked all my arguing out of me.

Finally I mutter, "Well, it's easy for you, 'cause you're good in gym."

Liat exhales loudly. "Gym isn't real life, Roxanne. Gym's going to be over one day."

"Well, real life stinks!" I say, and my lower lip quivers.

"Hey, no arguments there," Liat says.

I sniffle. "I don't get it."

"I don't either."

"But you're so tough. You know how to fight. You beat up Donna."

"You could learn that. It's no big deal."

"It is, too."

"Look, I told you. I'm Israeli. Like you. It's, like, an attitude thing."

"But I want to be American," I say in a small voice, and even as I'm saying it, I know that isn't a hundred percent accurate. Not anymore.

"You already are," Liat says, calling me on it. "Now, come on, let's find Kathleen."

I don't want to, but I follow Liat. Kathleen is sitting on my front stoop. When we come out, she says she's sorry for teasing me about my Lego romance.

"It's okay," I say, squirming, aware of Liat's eyes on me, but Liat doesn't say anything. She doesn't have to. Her eyes are saying it all: *You're too worried about people making fun of you.*

Kathleen suggests going to town for spice cakes. I go in the house to get Gayle. When Gayle and I come out, Eddie is standing next to Kathleen. My heart begins its normal being-around-Eddie pounding.

Eddie and Kathleen walk ahead of us. Every few minutes, Eddie leans over and tries to kiss Kathleen. Kathleen backs away from him every time and protests, "Eddie!" It's the kind of protest that sounds to me like, "Not right at this moment, hot stuff, but please try again later. Oh, and have a nice day!"

At last, Eddie succeeds in giving Kathleen a quick peck on the mouth before she can pull away from him. Kathleen giggles and slaps him playfully. I turn away, feeling sick. Liat's watching me. I avoid her eyes.

When we arrive at the bakery, we buy every spice cake they have in the display case. We each polish off two as we walk home. Eddie and Kathleen are ahead of us again. I'm growing very, very annoyed with them. Eddie is tearing pieces off his spice cake and feeding the chunks to Kathleen.

Suddenly, Kathleen bolts down the street. Eddie takes off after her. They disappear around the bend in the road.

By the time we reach them, they're leaning against the side of a house, making out like crazy. I can't help staring, taking in their closed eyes and the urgent way their mouths are moving. Eddie's arms are wrapped tightly around Kathleen, she's practically folded into him, and it gives me goose bumps to imagine my own body pressed against his instead of hers.

We pass them silently. When we reach our block, Gayle skips ahead.

Liat asks me, "How come you like Eddie so much?"

Somehow, I expected this question, but my face still flames with embarrassment. Is it that obvious?

"He's really cute," I reply dully. "He's, like, All-American." That simple sentence always seemed like enough of a reason to have a massive crush on Eddie. After I say it out loud, however, it sounds stupendously stupid.

Liat nods. "Yeah, Eddie is really cute in an All-American way."

I can tell there is more coming, and that it won't be good.

"But he's a jerk," Liat declares.

"You're right," I say without arguing. "He's a jerk."

chapter twenty

liat, gayle, and i sit on our stoop on a
Saturday afternoon, polishing off what's left of our
Halloween candy. After five Milky Ways, I decide I'm
never going to eat chocolate again.

"Do they have Milky Ways in Israel?" Gayle asks.
Her mouth is one great big brown smear. Nice.

Liat takes a big chomp out of a Snickers bar. "I'm
not sure," she says. "They might. There's all kinds of
Israeli candy bars, though."

"Elite, right?" I say.

"Yeah," Liat says, looking impressed.

"What's Elite?" Gayle asks.

"It's a brand of Israeli chocolate," I reply. "Like Hershey."

Gayle stares at me in mid-chomp. "How'd you know that, Roxanne?"

I try to act insulted. "I know something about being Israeli, Gayle." I'm just trying to annoy Gayle, but at the same time, I realize I really do know a lot about Israel—and I'm proud of that. I guess hanging out with Liat helps me remember all the things *Aba* and *Ema* taught me—the things I used to try to forget.

Gayle makes a face at me. With her mouth and fingertips smeared with candy bar, she looks like a chocolate alien from a distant Milky Way. Ha, ha.

"You guys are pretty good at speaking Hebrew, right?" Liat asks.

"Sure," we both say together. *Ema* and *Aba* have always spoken Hebrew to us, even if we do answer back in English. I guess it's one of those things we do without thinking, like breathing or blinking.

"There are these words that are really funny—the ones where two words are doubled. You know, like *koom-koom*."

"Teapot," Gayle says immediately.

Liat smiles at her. "*Par-par.*"

"Butterfly," I say, then in a moment of inspiration, "*Chach-chach.*"

"Lowlife," Gayle promptly translates, and we all crack up.

Eddie starts toward us from down the block.

"Speaking of lowlifes," Liat murmurs.

Gayle and I turn to her, then burst out laughing.

It's the first time I can remember making fun of Eddie like that. And my heart normally speeds up when Eddie is around, but I notice with some surprise that it doesn't now.

Kathleen is running to catch up with him.

"Anything going on?" Eddie asks when he reaches us. "Anything happening?"

"Nope," Liat replies.

"No deaths, no accidents, no dismemberments?"

"Nope," Liat repeats.

"Eddie," Kathleen scolds. "Cut it out."

Gayle offers them candy bars. They take them, even though she's muddied the wrappers with her sticky fingers.

"What were you guys talking about?" Eddie asks as he tears into a Three Musketeers, demolishing it in three bites. It's like watching a *T. rex* eat.

"Hebrew words," Gayle replies. "Do you want to learn some?"

"What's Hebrew?" Eddie asks.

"It's a language," I say. "It's what they speak in Israel."

"Huh," Eddie grunts, and I'm reminded again of a big stupid animal.

"I think it's cool that you guys know another language," Kathleen says, delicately peeling back her candy bar wrapper.

"You want to learn some Hebrew words?" Gayle asks again.

"Just the curses," Eddie replies.

We teach Kathleen and Eddie some of the Hebrew curses we know. They're pretty funny, actually. Kathleen gets them easily.

"I'm gonna use them at home," she says with a grin. "They won't have a clue. It'll be great."

But Eddie can't seem to get a handle on them at all. No matter how many times we enunciate the words for him, he can't get them through his thick head. He's massacring our language completely. Thinking of him as a *T. rex* was the right call after all, because his brain seems to be the size of a pea.

Have I been worshipping a big dumb oaf all this time just because he looks like an All-American guy?

chapter twenty-one

it happens in the middle of the night.

At 2:16 AM.

I'm groggy, still between the world of sleep and dreams, when I become aware of a curious red-orange light outside my window.

I hear loud noises that sound like bells. I turn over wearily and close my eyes. But the noises don't fade; in fact, they get louder. They sound like sirens.

And then I smell smoke.

I jump out of bed. When I peer out the window, I can hardly believe my eyes. Brilliant flames are licking the sky. Fire trucks, police cars, and ambulances, their red-and-blue sirens spinning madly, are parked at odd angles all over the street.

What I'm seeing finally connects with reality. I race down the hall, barge into my parents' bedroom, and find *Aba* standing at the window with a look of utter shock on his face.

"The Cursed House is on fire!" I scream.

I don't wait for a response. I bolt down the stairs and out the front door. It's only when I get outside that I realize I'm barefoot and in my flimsy pajamas with the hole in the seat of the pants.

The pavement feels like ice. It stings my bare feet. I half-run and half-stumble toward a crowd of people, all dressed like me, staring as if in a trance at the raging flames consuming the Cursed House.

The fire feels like an open oven. A heavy odor makes it hard to breathe. I wonder why the firefighters don't tell us to move back. I can't take my eyes off the dancing flames. It's like the fire is a living thing—rising, falling, rumbling like low thunder.

Aba and Gayle come out of the house and stand next to me. Gayle eyes the fire with a mixture of horror and wonder. *Aba* hands me a pair of fuzzy slippers. I absently slip them on my numb feet.

I become aware of Kathleen. She's holding Mikey in her arms. I recognize others in the crowd, too—Joe, Margo, Eddie.

But two people are missing.

The full realization of that hits me with a force so strong I actually stumble backward.

"Liat!" I yell, running forward.

Two firefighters hold up their hands to stop me.

"But my friend's in there!" I shriek.

My eyes burn, but I don't know if it's the smoke or the sudden terror I feel.

chapter twenty-two

the loss overwhelms me.

Not Liat.

Not strong, beautiful, tough, Israeli Liat.

I thrash violently against the firefighters, but they won't let me pass. They won't let me rescue Liat from the flames.

A growing pain inside me feels so sharp it's as though an invisible knife has reached into my very heart, splaying it open, leaving it bloody and mutilated.

"Roxanne! I'm here!"

I turn. Liat is standing to the side, away from the crowd, waving at me frantically. Her father stands behind her, bare-chested, his arms wrapped around her. Their eyes are red and puffy.

"Liat!" My relief is so strong it comes with a boatload of hot tears.

I run to her, wanting to squeeze her whole self to me—but when I get there, I'm overcome by a powerful shyness. Thankfully, Liat ignores it and pulls me into a smothering hug.

"Please clear the area!"

The firefighters are shooing us away.

"Please stay back. Please move away."

Some of the people in the crowd begin to go home. But Liat and I stay. We stand as close as the firefighters will allow us, holding hands, and watch the fire until it's over.

It isn't until the sun has risen over Brookfield Avenue that the fire finally dies down. By then, the fire trucks, police cars, and ambulances have left our block, crawling away as if in a parade. As sunshine illuminates the street, the extent of the damage becomes clear.

The Cursed House has burned to the ground.

Yet no other houses on the block, including the two on either side of it—ours and Margo's—have suffered any damage at all.

When I look at the spot, it's as if the Cursed House had never been there in the first place. All that's left is a charred foundation. In fact, when I try to remember what it looked like, I find my memory curiously blank. All I know is that it was bright pink.

≈ ≈ ≈

In the days following the fire, Liat and her father move into Rivka's apartment.

The Staten Island Fire Department cannot explain how the fire started. It wasn't arson, they say. It also wasn't an electrical malfunction.

In an article in the *Staten Island Advance*, the fire chief is quoted as saying, "I know this is going to sound funny, but we simply cannot find the cause. If you ask me, it's as if the house spontaneously combusted."

I remember learning about spontaneous combustion in science lab last year. A Radical Idea begins to form in my mind.

This Radical Idea starts out small but gets huge by week's end. It's so big, in fact, I can't get it out of my head.

See, everything I know about Liat, and the Cursed House, tells me it's absolutely right. But that doesn't mean I'm going to share it. Very few people would understand.

It's only when Gayle brings it up that I even say it out loud.

It's two weeks after the fire, and Gayle and I are walking home from school. We're silent most of the way until Gayle suddenly blurts out, "I think the Cursed House killed itself."

I inhale sharply. My teeth make a whistling sound. "I think so, too," I say.

I struggle to fashion my jumbled thoughts into coherent words. "I think that when Liat moved in . . . she . . . defeated the Curse. She beat it. So the Cursed

House . . . destroyed itself. And now, without it, there's no Curse anymore."

Gayle nods vigorously.

We never mention it again.

But some people on the block, like Eddie, don't see it our way.

They say the fire is only the latest example of the terrible reliability of the Curse. Even when we point out that no one got hurt in the fire and that the Cursed House itself is now gone, they insist the Curse struck again.

Some people even believe a new house will be built on that spot one day, and that it will be Cursed, too.

But they're wrong.

Gayle and I are right.

Even if a new house goes up on that spot one day, the Curse itself is gone.

Liat conquered it.

chapter twenty-three

it's almost thanksgiving now, and I've decided I won't let it be like Rosh Hashanah. Just because *Ema* can't be here doesn't mean we can't celebrate. And this year, we're going to have Israeli foods on the menu in addition to the traditional American foods. I'm going to make Old-Fashioned Yankee Spiced Cake— and *jachnun* too. I'm going to invite Liat, Yossi, and Rivka. It's going to be the best Thanksgiving ever.

I'm in my room, writing out the giant list of ingredients I will need from the supermarket. Liat's with me. We're both sprawled on the floor, blowing giant green bubbles that are collapsing stickily on our cheeks.

It reminds me of the first day I met Liat, that afternoon I saw her sitting alone on the stoop of the Cursed House, blowing big green bubbles.

Liat is unusually quiet. She scrapes three strands of gum off her face. "We're leaving, Roxanne," she says softly.

"What?" I ask absently.

Liat looks down at the floor. "We're going back to Israel," she says in a low voice.

I nearly choke on my wad of Bubblicious. *"What?!"*

Liat nods solemnly. Her face is pale.

"When?"

"In a couple weeks."

I can't find words. Finally I stammer, "But what about school?" It's a dumb question, considering everything.

Liat clears her throat. "I guess I'll go to school in Israel."

"No," I say. "You can't go. What about Thanksgiving?"

"I'm really sorry, Roxanne," she says sadly. Her eyes are shiny.

I blink back tears of my own. "But why?" I ask. Liat sighs. "My dad. He says it was a sign. He says it's time."

"A sign? You mean the fire?" I ask.

"Yeah," she says. "He says it's a sign that it's time we went back to Israel."

"But that's crazy!"

"I know. I tried talking him out of it, but when he decides we're moving, we're moving."

"But—," I start, then stop. The tears feel like they're about to gush. I blink furiously. "It's not a sign about Israel," I say, my voice breaking. "It has nothing to do with that. It's the Curse—it happens to everyone who lives in that house. Don't you know?"

I want to tell Liat she beat the Curse. I want to tell her about the Radical Idea—the house killing itself, the Curse being defeated. But all of a sudden, I can't say another word. I keep blinking, but I can't stop the tears. They rush out of my eyes, like a dam crumbling, streaming down my face.

Liat hugs me. "I don't want to go," she says.

My body shakes. "But what about gym?" I ask. Another stupid question.

Liat lets out a surprised snort. "Oh, Roxanne, forget about gym. You'll be fine in gym. Stop worrying about it."

But I do worry. I worry and cry. I cry until my tears

run dry. Liat and I hug and cling together until I think I can make her stay just by holding on to her. But I know I can't. And, when my tears run out, I don't feel better.

Instead, there is an empty place inside me that wasn't there before. It feels like an ache, a hole, just like the hole the Cursed House left when it burned to the ground. A hole in my heart.

Liat said losing someone hurts so much that everything else is nothing.

I get it now. *Ema*'s leaving stinks, but she's coming back—I know she is. This is different.

≈   ≈   ≈

Liat and her father stick around for two more weeks. But this short time Liat and I have together seems to disappear like a puff of smoke into air. Before I know it, it's actually time to say good-bye.

Good-byes are new to me. I've never really lost anyone, not like Liat has. Maybe I'm lucky.

A kind of numbness settles over me. I don't feel any sadness, just the permanence of that hole. I feel like I'm watching everything from the outside. I see myself watch Liat and Yossi pack their car. I stand silently as Kathleen and Gayle each give Liat a hug. I wait quietly as Liat approaches me.

"Write to me," Liat says.

I nod. But I wonder if Liat and I will really keep in touch. I think I needed her more than she needed me.

We hug for a long time.

Liat steps inside the car.

The last thing I see on the back of the rainbow zoo car as it heads to the airport is the picture Yossi painted—of Liat, Gayle, and me each blowing a giant green bubble.

I'm pulled out of my thoughts by Eddie's voice.

"Well," he says, making a cleaning motion with his hands. "Looks like the Curse strikes again."

I think about ignoring him. But I find myself saying, "And you're happy about it, aren't you?"

Eddie seems taken aback. "No," he stammers. "I'm not happy. I'm just saying—"

I don't let him finish. "You're a jerk," I say, and head into the house.

chapter twenty-four

liat's leaving is the bad news. *Ema*'s coming home in three weeks is the good news.

I don't understand how such an awful thing and such a wonderful thing can happen together at exactly the same time. One day I feel so sad, I think I will fall apart. Another day I feel so happy, I'm convinced I can fly. But, mostly, I feel different.

See, I think I finally figured some things out. The truth is, my parents aren't Carol and Mike Brady or Ma and Pa Ingalls. They never will be. If we still lived in Israel, though, *Ema* and *Aba* would speak the language perfectly, and my real name would be like everyone else's.

Is that better—to be like everyone else?

Liat would say no. Before Liat, I would've said yes.

I thought being American and being popular-cool-athletic were the same. But they're not. And I thought being Israeli was something to be ashamed of. But it's not.

And maybe—maybe—I can be American and Israeli at the same time. Like Liat.

I can try.

≈ ≈ ≈

In gym these days, we're playing more indoor Wiffle ball now that the weather's getting colder.

Today, Donna's captain. As usual.

Suri, Gheeta, and I are the last to be picked. As usual.

"Suri," I hear.

"Gheeta," I hear.

"Roxanne," I hear.

"It's Ravit," I say.

"What?" Donna snarls.

"Nothing," I reply. "It doesn't matter what you call me."

Donna scowls as I take my place with the team. Inwardly, I grin.

This time, it's me I see standing there, scarlet cape flaring out behind me, dark hair blowing in the wind.

I am a *sabra*, and I am American.

Y'alla.

author's note

why did i set this story in the 1980s?

Several reasons.

First, because of my own memories. I am a child of the era of Boy George, Rubik's Cubes, John Hughes movies, and Cabbage Patch Kids, and I enjoyed reliving the pop culture of my youth.

I'll also admit to another motive: lack of technology. If I had set the story today, I would have needed to incorporate an ever-changing array of twenty-first-century communications (email, texting, cells, Facebook, iPod, blogging). I wanted a story devoid of modern distractions, a story where TV reruns could actually be a part of a girl's coming-of-age (as they were for me), a story where kids could still gather outside on stoops.

Finally, our post–9/11 world makes any story involving Israel and the Middle East more complex than ever. While this subject has always been intricate, there was a time, believe it or not, when even that was a bit simpler.